MILAREPA: THREAT OR OPPORTUNITY

BY ROBERT D. GILMAN

ACKNOWLEDGMENT

Many thanks to my companions in the bars of North Beach through the years who kept me company and stocked my imagination for this story.

DISCLAIMER

Someone once bragged to me, "I would be ashamed to spoil a good story with facts." I have followed that policy in writing my novel. Of course, my experiences and the people I have known have gone into what I've cooked up, but also, there's been a lot of slicing and dicing and mixing up, adding seasonings and stewing, all for the sake of the story. One thing I do want to say: To the best of my knowledge, there has never been a Limbo Shift at the Saloon.

PROLOGUE

This is a story about Milarepa, Toni, me, and North Beach.

North Beach has a lot of sidewalks but no sand. There are almost no trees, but it's as easy to get lost there as in a forest. It's a confused place, one where people who don't really fit in fit in quite naturally. And so a place for Toni and for me.

As for Milarepa, the great medieval Tibetan Buddhist saint, his apparent reappearance right after the 9/11 terrorist attack didn't fit in either. It made a disturbing wave in the great world that also splashed over into North Beach.

The regular way to tell a story is to start at the beginning, go to the end, and stop. But in reality, life is always in the middle, so that's where I start – with Milarepa's reappearance, then back and forth. Back from how Toni died in my arms, our bumpy life with each other, to how out of nowhere we became tied together. Forth to how Toni, who after her death had been wandering in the bardo of becoming, came to Milarepa and how he transformed her into a Dakini with a sort of indefinite purpose to save the people of North Beach. About the Limbo Shift, an off and on after hours shift at the Saloon. Bill Quack, a bartender around North Beach who put out energy all over the place, had founded the shift, continued it after his death, then turned it over to Toni the Dakini, finally, how Toni grew the Limbo Shift and all the waves that made.

Who doesn't love to listen to the waves? Even when they're just washing up on the shore, you can feel the depth from which they come. There is surely a deep meaning there, but it hypnotizes concentration beyond explanation.

TABLE OF CONTENTS

CHAPTER 1 THE MILAREPA PHENOMENON

The earth wobbles on its axis. So does history, and it unbalances things in unpredictable ways -- -- some big things, some little things, some that are both. The reappearance of Milarepa and the movement that sprung up from that changed both. Who would have guessed that the kind of anxious and confused patriotism and jingoism that roiled through the country after September 11 would have ended up confronted, though confronted is not really the right word, by the mystical return of Milarepa, the great saint of ancient Tibetan Buddhism? Of course, as I've said, there's no agreement about whether he really did reappear. There's enough blah, blah blah to provide media filler items forever for slow news days. As for me, I found myself uncomfortably identifying with the bewildered straight in Dylan's old song: "Something is happening here; but you don't know what it is, do you, Mr. Jones?"

I was on a visit to Chicago, staying with old friends I'd made in college there back in the '60s. ***Milarepa: Threat or Opportunity*** I read on signs around the University of Chicago campus. It seemed like an opportunity to me. The University, some federal agencies, and some business groups had put together a week-long program with all sorts of lecturers making presentations. One of my drunken North Beach friends had written occasional religious stories for the San Francisco Chronicle; then, only a few months ago, become one of the frightening number of people who had suddenly given up the world for solitary meditation. I had asked him why, and he made no better sense to me than the articles I read about it. So much for insights gained from my personal circle.

He had brought his editor around the bars once, and I found the guy's card, gave him a call, and asked whether they had any interest in me writing up this conference for the Chronicle. "What the hell?" he said. "Give it a shot. Send me something, and we'll see." It looked like a way to pay for my plane fare, Maybe I'd even find somebody who would say something that would click.

Everybody knew the general outlines of the story more or less by osmosis. The Milarepa phenomenon had taken its place in the media alongside international tragedy, terrorism, politics, the economy, sports, and celebrities. You couldn't help sopping up the main outlines. Still, I got into the University of Chicago Library a few days before the big conference began and read enough to get the main outlines straight in my mind.

Milarepa apparently first turned up in Berkeley. Just how is foggy. You may remember various suspicious-looking aliens were interned after September 11, and apparently, one of them was a little naked green man who'd been sitting somewhere in the Berkeley hills meditating. He ended up in a cell with some six or seven other unfortunates who hadn't the good sense or good English to give a reasonable account of themselves. It was several days until they got around to processing them, and here the story takes its first odd turn. When they brought him forward and asked him who he was, instead of answering, the stories say, he asked, "Are the walls obstructive or nonobstructive?"

"Just tell us what your name is."

But instead of answering he walked straight through the outer wall next to him into the street. Outside, when police and National Guard poured out to give chase, he asked, "Is the air obstructive or nonobstructive?" And walked away back into the hills. Those trying to give chase said that the air congealed around them like molasses so that they could barely move.

There were some clerks or police who said they clearly heard these questions. None of them spoke anything but English. Among the other detainees, there were an Arab, an Indonesian, a Somalian, and a Pakistani. None of them had good English, but all heard him ask the same questions, but not in English, rather in the language each spoke. The story got a little play on the evening news. Nobody knew what to make of it, and the only follow-up was in the pages of the grocery store tabloids.

Naked men sitting off in the hills meditating aren't such a big deal in Berkeley, and there was nothing but a little local gossip for some time after that. Slowly, however, the rumor began that this was the Tibetan saint Milarepa, and he seemed to be acquiring a following. The Tibetan Studies Center in Berkeley heard the stories and decided to see if they could find him and put him to the test. He proved elusive. They'd think they had him spotted and knew where to go, but when they showed up with their interview team, video cameras, and microphones -- no Milarepa. It took two years before they talked one of the disciples he'd made into bringing Milarepa to see them. It led to the now famous "Song in a Garden."

It was a little garden in a small park in the East Bay hills. The Tibetan studies people were led there a little after dawn, where they found the little green man sitting naked in meditation in the misty grey light. He said nothing, did nothing while they arranged a small circle of chairs for themselves and set up their sound and video equipment. The leader of the group, a man of impeccable spiritual and academic credentials, addressed Milarepa, "As your disciple here has, I believe, explained to you, we have come here to meet you and ask you some questions about your practice."

The standard transcript continues thus:

I bow down to Marpa, the Translator.
I am the yogin Milarepa, blessed by my meditations to attain Enlightenment in this human life.
My song for you is simple: Do not be distracted.
My song is my green body
Turned green more than 1,000 years ago by eating nothing but boiled nettles.

My song is my naked body
Left naked because I concentrated only on Suchness.

The thieves who came to rob me in my mountain cave instead took pity on my poverty.
They came to steal from me,
Instead I took from them Illusion
For such of them who could as I
Be full with emptiness.

Do not be distracted.
Before your questions can be asked
My naked green body is the answer.
If I tell you answers, you will not know whether to believe me.
Instead, I abide in Suchness.

If I say that Suchness is one-pointed,
You will wonder how that is different from two-pointed or three-pointed.

You will think Suchness has a location and ask whether it
is inside or outside,
Up or down,
North, South, East, or West.

You will ask me about distinctions,
But I forgot all distinctions more than 1,000 years ago.
You will ask me about the true self,
But I know only Suchness.

Do not be distracted.
My song to you is my naked green body. This is Suchness.
Fill yourself with emptiness
And escape all distractions.

After Milarepa sang his song, there was a pause and then a
little shifting around among the delegation. Somehow, when the
leader was ready to go on, Milarepa had disappeared. There was a
search around the garden for him, but he was nowhere to be found.
The leader turned to the disciple who had arranged the meeting.
"Where is your Guru now? We have many questions for him."

"He has already answered your questions."

"But I thought he had agreed to speak with us."

"He has already spoken with you."

"This is no way to settle anything. Don't you realize that his
actions will only increase all the doubt and uncertainty that already
is clouding the great religious awakening that this might become?"

"Actions or inactions: doubt or certainty: heads or tails. The
only way to test the coin of Suchness is to bite and taste it." And
the disciple left also.

The shocking thing was that when the videotape was played later, the delegation leader's questions could be heard clearly, and various background noises -- birds, distant traffic, and so forth -- but Milarepa's song was completely inaudible though it did appear in subtitles on the screen. He was turned a little to the side so that his mouth could not be clearly seen. Yet there was an animation in his face as of someone speaking, and he gestured slightly with his head to emphasize certain points. The disciple could be clearly heard. Each of the auditors initially retained a clear memory of Milarepa's song, and these memories matched the subtitles on the video. Except that one French member of the delegation swore that the song had been in French and a Chinese scholar that it had been in Chinese.

The intent of the delegation had been purely spiritual and scholarly, but somehow, a copy of the videotape leaked out and wound up on the local news. Some treated it as a revelation, others as a hoax, and there was a falling out among the scholars as to what had actually happened, some declaring that the event was some kind of group illusion or hallucination, others somewhat reluctantly upholding the video as a genuine transcription of the event. Except, of course, that they maintained they had actually heard the song. The disciple refused to take the uproar seriously, saying that it was no more than a simple and plain manifestation of his Guru's teaching. Sixty Minutes later ran the tape with the caption, "Thoughts in a Garden: Green Thoughts from a Green Shade."

Milarepa hasn't been seen publicly since if, indeed, you think that he was, in fact, seen then, and if you count his arranged interview with the delegation as a public appearance. The little green man was seen no more in the East Bay hills. Rumors began to circulate that he had moved on to New Mexico. However, various disciples began to make their way to the forefront, claiming more or less direct contact with and/or inspiration from Milarepa. They ran a wide gamut from obvious hucksters to madmen to mainstream personalities turned in a new direction by the call of Milarepa's Suchness.

What really made the phenomenon, though was how a movement of people slowly took shape, as one by one many people abandoned their regular lives for solitary meditation in remote places. Though to call such an unorganized and individualistic process a "movement," perhaps is a misnomer.

The newspapers said 4% of the population of San Francisco had absconded to meditate, 3% of the total San Francisco Bay Area, 2.5% Los Angeles, and 1% San Diego. And it wasn't only California. New York, though starting late, claimed to have lost 1.5%, Chicago also 1.5%, Atlanta 2%, Houston and Dallas 1%, and St Louis 2%. Minneapolis was highest outside California at 3%. According to one article, if you put all the Reppies out in the wilds together in one metropolitan area, it would be a little larger than El Paso, Texas.

Despite checking various papers, magazines, and scholarly commentary, I never did read just where all these numbers came from. It isn't as if they had Census questions to go by. I think it must have come out of those marketing databases corporations are constantly buying and maintaining. So many from their sample were no longer at the same address, no longer buying whatever, and this projected out to the figures the papers used. But whatever the actual count, there's no question something real was happening. Everybody knew someone who'd packed up and gone sitting.

The bottom had dropped out of the real estate market in the cities and went out of sight in all sorts of isolated out of the way places. A friend once told me that one of Arizona's major industries after World War II had been real estate fraud. Now, both real and phony properties were selling like crazy. Arizona, New Mexico, West Texas, Iowa, the Dakotas, and Idaho all reported mini-booms.

Mail order meditation equipment became a big seller, and the U.S. Post Office all of a sudden had problems with the volume of mail going to remote spots. First, catalog orders came in; then the junk mail followed, but the "Reppies," as they began to be called, wouldn't pick up their ads. Finally, the Post Office began to hold quarterly regional bonfires for unclaimed junk mail, and the Reppies would come out for these as they would for nothing else. It seemed to be their one form of social gathering.

Many compromised and added meditation retreats onto their houses or apartments to which they'd withdraw for weeks or months at a time. The standard design was a room with an entrance hall added in. Friends or relatives would leave food and whatever other necessities had been agreed in the entrance hall. Afterward, the retreatant would come out, take the offering, and leave the trash to be disposed of. People preferred a bathroom built into their retreat, but some had to make do with one down the hall for which they were guaranteed their solitude during specified times.

The day the conference began, I walked into the conference hall, filled the shopping bag they gave you with literature from the various tables, and found myself a seat. While the keynote began, I flipped through the stuff I'd picked up and started reading a short biography of Milarepa.

Milarepa (1052 - 1135), the great saint of Tibetan Buddhism, spent his life in solitary meditation in remote mountain caves and such places throughout Tibet. Along the way, he brought Enlightenment to a multitude of local demons who subsequently became protectors of Buddhism. Although essentially solitary, he slowly became well known and attracted people to him, some out of curiosity, some seeking his teachings, some out of jealousy. His meditative songs had the power to open the third eye. His fame spread, and he gathered disciples. In the end, a jealous monk, unable to best Milarepa in dharma combat, poisoned him. Nevertheless, before his death, Milarepa brought his murderer to Enlightenment. The universe itself was moved by his passing, which was accompanied by a variety of miracles and wonders.

As a child, Milarepa and his mother were dispossessed of their inheritance by a greedy aunt and uncle. Mocking their weakness, the aunt said, "If you are many, raise an army. If you are few, use sorcery." His mother, steeled by this taunt, did indeed send Milarepa to learn sorcery. After a strenuous apprenticeship, he succeeded in casting spells, bringing disaster to his aunt, uncle, and their village supporters. However, his guru told him, "I taught you these spells; therefore, this evil karma belongs to me, and I may be reborn for many lives among the hungry ghosts if I do not immediately dedicate myself to overcoming it."

"But, Master," said Milarepa, "I thought that as an accomplished Guru, you had the knowledge to transmute bad karma into good, saving yourself and me, your disciple, from the endless chain of rebirth."

"In principle, I do," answered his Guru. "But in practice I have spent so much time on causing hail storms and such like spells that the details of transmuting karma have slipped away from me, and I fear my time remaining is too brief for me to bring them back."

In the end, they agreed that Milarepa, being still young, would go in search of the enlightening practices which would save both from the Wheel of Rebirth. Milarepa found Translator Marpa. Marpa had Milarepa build towers for him, hauling great rocks with his slight body; then, when the tower was finished, he changed his mind and had Milarepa take it all down again, stone by stone and rebuild it elsewhere. Milarepa, downcast, tried to escape, but his fate was otherwise. In the end, he broke through his sufferings to attain Enlightenment. Marpa informed him then that his destiny would be to spend his life in meditation in the wild places of Tibet, saving sentient beings by his austere practices.

The conference keynote was a crashing bore, as those things so often are, and unfortunately, a presage of things to come. There was economic analysis: could meditation be priced as an equivalent value to its alternatives in the lives of the Reppies, and so counted in the Gross Domestic Product? Was it democratic or a threat to democracy? The Reppies didn't vote, but on the other hand, they didn't riot in the streets either. It was sensitive internationally. Early on, the Dalai Lama had been pressed for comment but limited himself to saying only that Milarepa was indeed a great saint and that the manifestation of the meditative spirit could be a way of spiritual realization for those who chose to pursue it. Nevertheless, China had interpreted it as a veiled threat to their claims on Tibet. Fundamentalists thought it was an outrage to Christianity, but religious liberals saw it as at once an extension of the Judeo-Christian spirit and a return to ancient Christian hermetic traditions. The only Buddhist on the program was a Zen teacher who maintained that Milarepa had slighted Bodhidharma, the Zen Patriarch who brought the dharma from India to China. He devoted 40 minutes to nursing this ancient grievance which no one there but he had ever heard of before. He probably generated more sympathy for the Reppie phenomenon than any other speaker.

Listening to these presentations, you'd never have guessed that something had happened which had drastically changed the lives of several tens of thousands of people and had mothers and fathers around the country scared shitless as great generational changes so regularly do.

I thought of my friend, the former drunk and religious journalist, now gone sitting, and my last conversation with him. "You've been going back and forth to work and to the bars for 15 years. Why do you suddenly want to go sit by yourself in the wilderness?" He'd drawn a big circle on the table with his damp beer glass, then dotted the center. He pointed to the center. "This is what I need," he said. I sighed. "You wrote a really funny column about all this just three months ago." He'd just shrugged and smiled. If he'd been on form and covering this program, he would have written something very excited, taking all the implications to their extremes and staging a boxing match among them. As for me, I found a little amusement in one minor lecture and wrote it up.

The speaker was a mathematician, an otherworldly man. He at least had been touched by Milarepa and, in a quirky way, had worked his questions into the fabric of his life. He'd expressed a curiosity about the Reppies to a friend who taught "Cross-Cultural Dimensions of Religion." This friend had given him The Hundred Thousand Songs of Milarepa, a massive compilation of Milarepa's exploits during his travels, meditating in remote places all over Tibet. "Of course, I saw at once that at 900 pages of text, there would have to be more than 100 songs per page, counting in the ordinary way, and a glance was sufficient to show that, even though there were quite a number of songs, many of them covered multiple pages so that I doubt if there were even 800 songs. That led me to consider packings of self-similar objects, a sort of fractal structure, as a possible better way of understanding it. Of course, in such structures, the whole is self-repeating to numberless miniature levels and numberless larger levels so that, really, the whole cannot be grasped in its entirety, only a sort of limited slice with a horizon up and down of so many levels. (I must say I find our ordinary ways of assigning quantitative measures using natural numbers counterintuitive for thinking about these kinds of things. However, I fear I have not found a satisfactory alternative yet.) It seems evident that, really,"100,000 songs" is not meant as an exact specification but only to point to a very great many; more than one is able to be taken in at once. Now, of course, this is just my initial speculation. I lack the linguistic knowledge -- and I gather that there really is not an established definitive text -- which adds all sorts of historical and critical difficulties to any effort to test these ideas systematically. But I must say that personally, I find this a very intriguing line of inquiry and have some regrets at having come upon it so late in life when it is not really possible for me, in the time I have left, to pursue the matter to any real depth or with any rigor." He had, however, gone on to some further review of Buddhist concepts and discovered geometric significance in the eight fold path and the four noble truths. "The regular octagon and the square together tile the plane; that is to say, form an infinite covering. This, of course, is a familiar concept, and the plane a familiar device for representing, say, time along one axis, and distance along another. Considering the various axes of symmetry, rotations, reflections, and transgressions. uh, rather, translations have their interest, and, I believe, liberates one from simple unidirectional thinking and reveals diversity within conformity. However, we are not constrained to a simple view of two or three dimensions. It is the eightfold path, after all. When we begin to consider folding along the various axes, and the inter-relations thereby created, we begin to perceive things which are different from those available in our ordinary representations of space and time." He proceeded to take from his briefcase three or four complex origami models, each model with pieces showing both the various construction stages, and with the various vertices and edges carefully labeled for reference. The rest of his lecture went into the technical details of folding the eightfold path. He'd broken it all down so that you could follow at each step how he got from there to the next one, but the lecture as a whole, I'm afraid, was completely incomprehensible to me.

I think that would have been it for Milarepa and me if Toni hadn't turned up. Toni had no business being here. She had lived her life as if it were a bucking bronco, getting back up on it after each toss. But it never gentled for her and had done for her eight years ago now. She had actually died in my arms as I carried her 88-pound body from the futon sofa in the living room back to the hospital bed. The Hospice people had set up in the empty bedroom in my apartment. It was the same apartment I'd thrown her out of two years before that.

This day in Chicago, I'd thought I'd seen her earlier in the day, or rather had said to myself in a distracted sort of way, how much the woman dancing down at the Point had looked like her. The lakefront in Chicago always picks me up. While the conference was winding up that afternoon, I'd taken a walk down 55th Street to the lake and down along the rocks that line the lake. There'd been a crowd gathered around some bongo players; there were also a couple of flutes, a lot of clapping, and a woman dancing in the middle. I could just glimpse her now and then through the crowd. She was something else. Barefoot on the rocks there and naked except for some sort of shimmering diamond patterned snakeskin thing coiled loosely two or three times around her torso. It ended behind her back in a little peacock feather fan that whipped around first over her head then down to her ass as she danced. "Looks just like Toni," I'd said to myself idly, and went on with my walk. Later in the hall before the closing conference session I overheard some people talking about "the naked lady down at the Point." They seemed to find her much more interesting than the Milarepa conference.

That evening, I had a final dinner with my friends, and then, back at their place, I packed in preparation for flying back to San Francisco in the morning. That done, I stretched out in the spare room my friends had given me and turned the light off. Their apartment was just off 53rd Street, and a big neon sign there cast pulses of red light through the window curtain in a kind of spotted and netted pattern against the wall. The breeze through the window moved the curtain and made the light pattern shiver and twist. I fell into a kind of reverie. The moving, pulsing spots on the wall seemed to condense and move away from the wall into the peacock tail pattern of the dancer at the Point. Light seemed to collect and radiate from the dancer's snake skin coils. Then the entire snake's tail coils unwrapped cracked the peacock fan at me like the tip of a whip, coiled back up, and there was Toni standing in front of me.

"That should wake you up," she said. "Pay attention." And she came over and gave me a quick kiss. I sat up. "What the hell are you doing here?" I asked. "You're dead. And where did you get that weird tail?"

"I'm a Dakini now," she said proudly. "Milarepa, Millie I call him, made me one. It's been really strange. I'm still trying to figure it all out. I mean, I think I'm a Dakini, but I might be a demoness; I can't be positive. But I really think I'm a Dakini. And anyway, Millie's been a big help, so when I saw you here, I had to come see you. I got distracted this morning by the music down by the lake, but here I am."

"You remember what I kept teaching you about the Hanged Man in the Tarot deck? About how it wasn't just death; it wasn't just negative; it was also change. And you know me -- always the do - don't girl - I was always flip-flopping about whether I loved or hated my life. So, in a way, I was all primed when I died and ready for the next step. Well, horse on me. You know there's supposed to be the Bardo of Becoming for a few days after you die and before you get on with it? Well, I got stuck there like it was some kind of damn North Beach bar that I didn't like but couldn't get out of. It was like I was stuck in an after-hours party, and I was the only one who realized how boring everybody was."

I was drawn in despite myself. "I read about that, Bardo," I said. "It said that the phase after death is the reawakening of consciousness, experiencing the fantastic projections of the mind, hallucinations produced by the mind disconnected from the fabric of day-to-day existence. No wonder you got stuck there. You couldn't tell the difference from your ordinary life. "

Toni thought for a moment. "Maybe," she said. "Whatever. Anyway then after a long time, I heard about Millie, and I decided to go see for myself. So I went and circumambulated him while he was meditating. I think you're only supposed to do it three times, but I did it seven, and then I did three prostrations in front of him. And while I was walking around him, this tail started to come out, and when I did my prostrations, the peacock feathers on it. And there I was, a Dakini. I did three more prostrations and split. I always knew I had the most fantastic tail in the world. Look."

She uncoiled her tail and stretched it out in front of me, leaving her thin body uncovered with its tiny tits, big dark nipples, and nicely curved hips and ass. The tail was silver grey and black in large diamonds, and the scales shimmered. The peacock feathers started out of the top third of it and reached maybe 14 inches beyond the tip of the tail. She brushed my cheek with the feathers. "Quit teasing me, Toni." She giggled and wound her tail back around her body.

"But what did Milarepa teach you?" I asked.

"Weren't you paying attention? He turned me into a Dakini."

"But didn't he say anything to you? Didn't he give you instructions or something?"

"Just turning into a Dakini was as much Enlightenment as I could handle right then. I mean I'm still figuring out how to deal with it. The way I understand it, I'm supposed to be a guardian spirit now, but I don't know how. How do you protect North Beach people from anything? Sometimes I'd try to tell people for their own good while I was alive, but it never did anything. It was like you remember I used to talk to the TV shows and try to warn the people how to stay out of trouble. My advice did just as much good. So what am I supposed to do now as a Dakini? I don't know. I just went off in the desert to paint. All those reds and browns and yellows and turquoise. I got way the hell away from everybody, and I've been tripping out just making stuff. Then I saw you here, and I said, 'Well, at least I should say hello.' I mean, if you were wondering about Millie, I could clue you in. "

I shook my head and put it down on my arm. "Toni, you know I don't believe in spirits and Dakinis and all that. Why are you doing this to me? I don't understand this Milarepa stuff, but all you're doing is making everything more confused."

Despite what I said, I knew it really was Toni. Her physicality and spirit were all knotted together, giving her a presence at once intense, immediate and intimate, and I recognized it. And she was always doing unpredictable stuff.

Toni came over and laid her small hand on the back of my neck. "Poor, baby, you still don't have a clue how to pay attention. That's what I was always good for you for is to make you more confused. You think you need to be unconfused but it just bores you. I'm confused too. Maybe I'm really a demoness instead of a Dakini. But I don't think so. Because of what I feel when I'm dancing. It's lots of power but it's not demoness power, it's Dakini power. "

I jerked my head away. "Fuck you and your magic tricks. I'm not Dante. I don't need to be saddled with some kind of New Age speed shooting Beatrice, trying to save me by making fun of reality."

Toni shimmered a violent red, and I'd swear shot a black ray out of her eyes. She turned her back on me, and all sorts of nervous colors trembled around her. Then she got a kind of deep purple and pink going that she managed to steady herself with. She turned back around, "Don't do that to me again, baby," she said. "I'm going to show you. It's another part of how I know I'm a Dakini, part of what happened when Millie changed me. " She stepped up close to me and stretched the inside of her forearms out in front of me. "Look, baby, no tracks. "

It was a tremendously intimate gesture. In the old days Toni would expose any part of her body before she'd show her forearms where the track marks were. "I didn't mean it," I said. I pulled Toni's arm to me and kissed the inside of her elbow.

She patted my head with the other hand, then pulled away and stepped back. She uncoiled her tail from around her body, recoiled it on the floor, and sat down on it, leaving her body bare. "Keep calm," she said. "I'm not coming on to you. I just have to sit down. You've got to get used to seeing me like this."

"I never did get used to you before, Toni. I don't know why I should be any better at it now."

"I didn't come here to make you believe anything you don't want to," she said and thought a moment. "We never did see the same thing as reality anyway. I mean, we did, and we didn't. Is it so important?"

"You can't just be from Missouri, you know. It's a big world, and everybody sees lots of different things; and, if you could only talk about just what you'd see for yourself, you wouldn't have much of anything to talk about. Or much of anybody to talk to either."

"It's like we're all linked up hand in hand, and the chain stretches around the corner, and you have to get the report on what's around the corner from the people up there. . . and around the corner of the corner, and so on. It gets to be like that party game where you start a story at one end, then wait and see how fucked up it becomes after it gets repeated down to the other. Except, of course, that you just don't have the way to find out for sure what the original story was. And there's a lot of cross-talk.

And, of course, you can't trust what some people say no matter what."

"We can still talk, baby. You don't have to believe me any more than you ever did."

I just looked at her and shook my head.

"I better go," she said. "Watch." She stepped back into the room, shimmering in the pulsing light from the neon sign with the patterns from the curtains blown across her form. She flicked her tail out, then wound it up again, twirling as she did so, and disappeared with a final flick of the peacock tail, leaving just the neon light making patterns on the wall again.

CHAPTER 2 TONI TAKES THE LIMBO SHIFT

Back to San Francisco. That night in Chicago after Toni disappeared, somewhat to my surprise, I went to sleep without any trouble and had strange, pleasant dreams, none of which I can remember. On the flight back, I had the murder mystery I'd bought to read sitting open in my lap, but couldn't bring my attention to it. I thought very little about Milarepa but a lot about Toni.

I had told her I don't believe in spirits and so forth, and I don't, but she, who had seemed to live in a kind of life-and-death Never-Never-Land, nevertheless had always been immediate and real to me, though always in a startling kind of way. And so she seemed now, a kind of wake-up call if l was asleep or a dream intrusion waking, and I found it was beyond me to take up the question of whether she really existed now as a Dakini. Instead of any sort of orderly going over Milarepa and Toni's sudden appearance, I just found myself replaying the times she had appeared and disappeared into and out of my life.

And so it went through the week to the following Sunday morning when I got up at six and walked down to the bar for my morning coffee. That's one of the great things about North Beach. There are bars open at six AM. Over the years, I've switched back and forth among them to start my day. I figured out long ago that I preferred being around a bar and maybe a few people finishing up the night before to sitting in a company cafeteria with a bunch of other people about to go to work. I recall just about the first time I went to Vesuvio for my morning coffee. There were two guys in there, still drunk from closing Gino's the night before. One of them had busted a knuckle on his right hand shooting pool. He'd swung the cue so hard, making the initial break, that it had slammed into the table. When Gino's closed, he and his buddy had just time to get a pint of something to nurse them through the small hours until Vesuvio opened up. He was toughing it out, waiting until he could make it to work, have an accident to bust the knuckle there, go to the ER, and so get workers' comp to cover it. It was a hare-brained sort of scheme based on a kind of naïve innocence about how his boss at work would react. I don't know how it came out. I don't think I ever saw either of those two again. But I decided I preferred the kind of wild and woolly world of the bar to the company cafeteria in the morning, where the impending workday cast a serious and glum shadow over the mood.

On the weekends, I'd start with coffee, then see what that led to.

During the week, Alice Tall tended bar, Friday and the weekend, Phoenix – or Firebird as she mostly preferred. What a pair to draw to, as they say.

Alice Tall was half of The Alice. She was big, boozy, and friendly and had a kind of casual and slightly worn sexiness to her. Tall used to hum to herself a little while she tended bar. Her inner world was never too distracted by her customers, but, somewhat to my surprise, she was only occasionally too distracted to check that people had the drinks they wanted in front of them.

Alice Small was the other half of The Alice. The nicknames came from the song "The White Rabbit":

> One pill makes you larger
> And one pill makes you small
> And the ones that mother gives you
> Don't do anything at all

Go ask Alice
When she's ten feet tall

And if you go chasing rabbits
And you know you're going to fall
Tell'em a hookah smoking caterpillar
Has given you the call
Call Alice
When she was just small

When men on the chessboard
get up and tell you where to go
And you've just had some kind of mushroom
And your mind is moving slow
Go ask Alice
I think she'll know

When logic and proportion
Have fallen sloppy dead
And the White Knight is talking backwards
And the Red Queen's off with her head
Remember what the dormouse said:
"Feed your Head
Feed your Head!"

The Alice lived in a small room in a cheap residence hotel, the Tevere. They called it the Crow's Nest. There wasn't much room - - barely more than space for a twin bed for each, a closet, a chest of drawers, and a table with a couple chairs. What made it was the triangular corner with the big bay window that looked down over the Columbus and Broadway intersection. Years ago, Badges had built up a platform in the window alcove that came up almost to the bottom of the window. It was covered with a nice thick rug, and Badges had completed it with guard rails to keep you from falling out the window. They had cushions there, and it was a classic place to have some beers, smoke grass, and stare out over North Beach. At one point when I was on vacation and didn't have to go from Vesuvio to work, Tall brought me up there after her morning shift. There was an unsteady stream of The Alice's friends in and out through the day, most in the window socializing, but also, someone crashed on one of the beds. After that introduction, I'd come up from time to time to visit.

The Crow's Nest had an extra door propped against one wall. It had been the door in the Alice's prior apartment. They had brought the door with them when they moved into the Crow's Nest because of Billboard Fred's painting done long ago of Tall, Small, and Tall's kids. It had been painted not too long after the final convulsions of the Symbionese Liberation Army. It showed Tall taking up most of the door, smiling with a drink in one hand and a stoned sort of grin on her face. Small came only up to Tall's hip. She was in a Patty Hearst/Tania style revolutionary pose with an AK-47 in one hand, the other arm hooked around one of Tall's giant thighs. Small had a Cobra wrapped around her waist with the hooded head looming just above her own. Tall's two kids were there from when they were still quite little, the older one holding onto Tall's other leg, the younger holding hands with the older with one hand, the other holding onto Small's trouser leg. The painting was really partly a joke. Small, to be sure, was full of revolutionary convictions, but nobody took her rants very seriously. Tall didn't care about convictions. She'd mostly think whatever you liked. But despite her passivity she always seemed the bigger force.

That Saturday in Vesuvio, the Duke of Dark Corners was already there, sitting in the corner where I'd usually sit and read the paper. He and Firebird were talking. I took my place on the stool next to him. "Hey, Duke, I see you're looking sharp this morning."

His dark brown skin and dark blue suit blended into the corner, but the bright red tie and big gold ring let you know he was there. "Robert," he nodded, "I been to the crap house, and I like to look sharp there. It's a many years since I been to church, and I gots to look sharp sometime. The Lord knows I left more money in the crap house than my mother-dear left the preacher, and she left him a lot."

The Duke had a lot of nicknames. "Wiley Coyote, King of the Road, Duke of Dark Corners." Wiley Coyote because of his first name and the flamboyant way he carried himself. King of the Road because of the way he shuffled cars in and out of the parking lot he'd taken care of all the years I'd known him. Duke of Dark Corners I'd given him because of his habit of sitting in the dark corners in the bars and because I'd always loved the line in Measure for Measure where Licio, the unbridled reprobate, all unknowingly, insultingly praises the supposedly absent Duke. He does so, of course, to the Duke himself, who is in disguise checking out how the city gets along without him. Licio derides the harshness of the deputy left in charge of the city. "This had not happened with the fantastical old Duke of dark corners." I loved the line and the play situation, and to me, it seemed natural for our own barroom Duke. The nickname took, adding itself to the list of titles the Coyote carried, though in practice, everyone, me included, shortened it to just "the Duke."

"Where you been?" he asked. "You mostly be here every morning."

"Visiting in Chicago," I said. Then, not seeming to be able to help myself, I added. "I saw Toni there."

"Say what?"

"I saw Toni there. I went to this Milarepa conference, and at the end of it, Toni turned up. She said Milarepa turned her into a Dakini after she died. She's got a great big snake's tail now with peacock feathers at the end of it."

The Duke pursed his thick lips together the way he did when he was considering something. Then he said, "Robert, I have to compliment you telling me something like that when you ain't even had nothing but coffee to drink."

I didn't say anything for a moment. I took another swallow of my coffee and almost went back to reading the paper. But in the end I found I had to go on. The Duke always knew everything going on up and down the street. Partly, it was because he was out on the street all day parking cars and talking to people, then in and out of the bars up and down the street refreshing himself. The other part was because everybody confided in him.

"I know it sounds ridiculous. But when you think about it, it's not any stranger than the other stuff she used to do. She said she's supposed to be a guardian spirit for the people of North Beach now, but she didn't know how, so she's been off painting in the desert. "

The Duke went through his lip-pursing routine again before he spoke. He called the Firebird over. "Get Robert a cocktail. I believe he needs one to straighten out his concentration."

"Robert, Toni was one crazy lady. She drove you crazy living, and you went along with it. Now, here she is again, so you say, and it's up to you again."

"I tell you one thing. If she went off to paint instead of saving the people of North Beach, at least she showed some sense for a change."

"I been done a lots of things for these people on these streets, but I'm going to tell you it's no help. If l had all the money I so called loaned to these people, I wouldn't never have to worry no more. Getting help weren't no help to me neither. Remember how I used to borrow off you $20, $50. Then one day you told me, 'I ain't loaning you no more. You got a job.' Which was true. I didn't need it, but I borrowed it anyway. And especially I didn't need it since I always paid it back. It was just better for me without. And tell the truth that's really how you help people. But ain't no point to tell them that. And if it don't help them, at least it helps you."

"I think she's still working out how to be a Dakini."

"Don't be in no big hurry to get her explanation because I seen Toni start a lots more things than I seen her finish. I thought she got finished with her life, but from what you say, I guess she's just changed costumes again for that."

"But I ain't going to say no more. Most probably, I already said too much. There's two rules not to tell people about and that's their religion and their lady, and I guess I more or less broke both of them. Just don't take me too seriously. I used to think my mother-dear was a religious fool, which I expect she thought I'd more or less gone to hell, but when I really messed up and needed help, she did it. And she said it was for her religion she did it. So it did me some good, even if it was more for me than her religion she did it. I said from then it ain't no point to disrespect somebody's religion so long as it ain't hurting you and most especially not when it's helping you. Robert, there's a lots of people in this world smarter than me; and they's a lot of them, what they believe don't make me no sense. But they ain't asked me. And even if they do I wouldn't tell them, being as I'm in the business of getting tips from them."

That sounded like a line to end the conversation. But so many barroom conversations carry right by over a full stop again and again. I've listened to them and been in them, and I wasn't ready to stop yet. And I think the Duke's speech was more by way of a disclaimer than a real effort to turn off our talk.

"I don't know how I'm going to handle it if she's back here hanging around," I said.. "I mean, do Dakinis need a place to stay? She can't stay anywhere without taking it over and making it her own chaos. But I don't think I could stand to see her in the street either. I don't know what she thinks she's got to do to be a guardian spirit."

"Robert, one way or other, you gots to live your life. You want to start a Daiquiri hotel, or whatever you may call it, that's your life. You want to keep hitting the bars and getting drunk. That's your life. You want to go be a Reppie, then that's what you want to do. You want to save the people of North Beach, then you're crazy, but the people here don't mind that, and that's your life too."

And that was a sign-off. The Duke slapped a five-dollar tip for Firebird under his empty drink and strutted off to hit another bar. I turned off my thoughts and read the paper.

On Sunday. I showed up a little past 6 AM to see Phoenix standing outside in the fog, sharing a joint with Lucky Bob. The little spots of light reflecting in the fog gathered here and there in her red hair and echoed at the tip of the joint she and Lucky Bob passed back and forth.

"Morning, Bobby," she said. "Want a toke? No? Well, go ahead inside and sit. Coffee's coming down. I'll be there in a second. Just let me finish preparing myself here."

"All prepared?" I asked when she came in and poured my coffee.

"I'm never prepared, Bobby. Especially not after last night. You'd think I'd know better by now, but I'm too big a ship. Once I get my momentum going, it carries me straight past closing time."

She poured herself a shot of Fernet and knocked it back, making a face. "Foul stuff, but it does pick you up," she said. "Thank God for morning shifts where good people like you will cut me a little slack. If I didn't have to get up and go to work in the morning, God knows if I'd ever get up. They might as well let the hearse be my taxi cab. I actually heard a guy tell the bartender that one night.

'Bartender, please call me a hearse.' "

"So you were out and about last night, Phoenix?"

"I was out for the count last night, Bobby." She slugged down another shot of Fernet. "But call me Firebird, Bobby, Firebird. Rising from the ashes. Which is what my mouth tastes like. Even Fernet tastes better than my mouth this morning."

"So did you see the little Mormon guy?" I asked.

"What little Mormon guy was that?"

"He was here in Vesuvio when I came in last night. Last time I saw him, he was passed out in a corner at the Saloon."

"Passed out?" Firebird looked puzzled. "Mormons don't drink."

"I guess he must have forgotten that after the first three or four. He came in here in a suit and tie with a couple of other guys I never saw before. Apparently, they just got out of some kind of convention. He was having Coca-Cola with them; then they left, but he decided to stay. He was sitting next to Slick Joe. He asked Joe whether he knew that God watches us all. Then he started telling him about how Mormons had to do missionary duty, going out among the heathen and spreading the word of God. And he thought maybe the ladies calling him into the topless joints were a voice from God to deliver the message of salvation into North Beach. Then his convention mates had hauled him into the bar, and he thought it was like he'd been summoned into the jungle and it was his duty to pull the people here out of the devil's maw. So Joe asked him did he want a drink. And this guy explained to him that Mormons didn't drink; that drink was the bait on the hook the devil used to pull souls to hell."

Joe told him that if he wanted to pull the people here anywhere, he'd have to gain their confidence, and we don't have any confidence in anybody without a drink in their hand. Then he said if drinks are the devil's bait, and God had shown the Mormons the way, maybe God could show how to just nibble the bait off the hook and leave the devil crying. Then he told him as how Chartreuse is made by monks from a secret formula passed down the ages. Randy was behind the bar, and he put a rocks glass full of Chartreuse in front of the guy fast as a miracle from God."

"The little guy kind of steeled himself. Then he said, 'I know what you're trying to do. But with God, all things are possible.' And he threw the whole thing down. Then he made faces and swallowed two or three times, straightened his back, and looked proud of himself. Randy just poured him another. He stared at it, nodded his head two or three times, made a big grimace, lifted the drink off the bar and held it in front of his face for about ten seconds, then threw the second one down. More faces, more swallows; then, a silly grin, and 'With God, all things are possible. 'He studied the end of his nose a bit. Then he told Randy, 'I'm going to show you people here the mighty works of God. I want you to give everyone here one of these drinks, and I'm going to show you how God defies the devil.' Randy explained to him how everybody had their own particular thing that they drink; was that all right? 'With God, all things are possible.' So Randy poured out drinks for the bar and another Chartreuse. Told him he was going to give him the round for $50. The Mormon guy blinked two or three times but pulled out his wallet, studied inside, smiled like he was the King of Persia, and put three twenties on the bar. 'I'm going to show you to bibble the Bevil's bait,' he said and swallowed another one."

"I drank my drink and went out to eat; then, I was up and down the street checking out the bars. I didn't see him again. But I heard Slick Joe stuck with him and was touring him up and down the street, helping him empty his wallet. Like I said, last I heard of him, he was passed out in the Saloon."

The phone rang. "Firebird, here, up and out of the ashes. Don't ring that phone so loud at me. ... O, hi, baby. Been hearing rumors about you but haven't seen you in a long time."

"... You got the Limbo Shift? I thought that was Bill Quack's.

"... Well, yeah, I know how he gets in his moods and leaves things. But you, Toni, you could match anybody mood for mood. What is it? A qualification for the shift? ... Yeah, Rainier Bob's here. OK, I'll tell him."

Firebird hung up the phone and told me, "That was Toni. Said she's taking over the Limbo Shift at the Saloon and for you to come up and see her when you finish your coffee."

"Limbo Shift? What are you talking about?"

"You never heard about the Limbo Shift? I'm surprised. Well, Toni says she's got it now, so just go on down there, and she'll tell you."

I headed out across Broadway for the Saloon. It bills itself as San Francisco's oldest bar, "Established 1861," and looks the part. Old wood building sitting at Grant and Fresno Alley. Dark inside. Nothing new. Big old wood back bar. Big oil paintings up near the high ceiling, so covered over with smoke by now, it's mostly a guess what's in them. Some ghostly figures in some sort of landscape. Toni had pulled a bar stool back behind the bar and was sitting in the middle near the cash register. One leg was crossed over the other, and her tail wound around her body with the peacock fan mostly folded in and resting against a cheek. Slick Joe and Bill Quack were down toward the end of the bar, working on drinks. Seeing me, Toni pushed herself off the stool, went to the beer box at the door end of the bar where I was now standing, and pulled a Rainier Ale out of it for me. "Hey, baby," she said. "Look. I got Rainier for you."

"Firebird said you've got the Limbo Shift, but I've got no idea what that is."

"Well, Bill Quack used to do it; in fact, he started it, but he says he's tired of it now. So I'm going to take it."

"Bill's been dead ten years at least."

"I told you it was the Limbo Shift. Weren't you listening?"

I took a pull of my Rainier. Rainier Ale had become my regular drink shortly after I arrived in North Beach, so much so that I became known as Rainier Bob – to distinguish me from Lucky Bob (who drank Lucky Lager and Specs Bob, who tended bar at Specs. Rainier Ale was nicknamed "the Green Death." It reminded me of that verse in the Cocaine Blues,

Cocaine's for horses, not for men.

They say coke will kill you, but they don't say when.

"Hard to find Rainier in the bars these days," I said. "I wonder when Damian started stocking them again."

"Damian didn't start stocking them again. In fact, Damian doesn't have anything to do with the Limbo Shift. Bill worked it out with Nappy when Nappy owned the bar. Nappy turned it over to Bill, and now Bill's turned it over to me. And I put the Rainier in for you. So act right, or I'll put you on Budweiser."

"I don't understand what's going on."

"It started when Bill was working up the street at the Lost and Found on the weekends, and Big Sam was working here. Sam and the doorman and usually some of the musicians would sit around in the back here after hours talking and winding down. And Bill would come along after a while from the Lost and Found and pound the door till they let him in. Then they'd all start gabbing. One night he brought his cocktail waitress with him, and you know

how he can't keep still. He wanted to open up the bar. They told
him he couldn't; it was after hours." He told them, "Fuck after
hours. This is limbo. And if you can't have a drink in limbo, where
can you?" And he went ahead and served everybody a round. They
were all fucked up in twenty minutes. Then Nappy came by, heard
the party going on inside, used his keys to open up, and started
yelling what was going on. Fortunately, he had a heater on himself
at the time, and Bill poured him a big Jack Daniels, told him
everything was alright because it was the Limbo Shift, and Bill
would take full responsibility. You never could tell with Nappy.
He went for it. Bill even had some of the street winos in here and
was pouring drinks for them. They must have thought they'd gone
to heaven. Bill couldn't find anybody else that time in the morning,
and he had too much of a high going to be happy with just a few
regular drunks around him.

"So that's how it started, and Bill kept it up every now and
then after. Then he died and didn't have much of anything else to
do, so he started doing the Limbo Shift more and more. He'd just
open it up anytime he felt like it, and there wasn't any other
bartender working. It's a great shift. Bill pulled them all in --
living, dead, whatever -- it never made any difference to him. And
now he's given it over to me."

"So this is how you're going to save the people of North
Beach?"

"Who has more influence with them than their bartender?"

I looked down the bar to Bill Quack and yelled out the line
that had regularly greeted him in his life when he came on his
shifts, "Is there a Doctor in the house?"

Bill looked at me, not really into it, but he went ahead with his standard answer: "Yes, but he's a quack. Quack, quack, quack, quack, quack." He broke after the first couple quacks into his Donald Duck voice. He gave out, tipped his glass toward me, killed his drink, and waved it at Toni for another.

I called to Slick Joe, "What did you do with your Mormon?"

"I had a shift to work at the Columbus. I passed him on to Captain Marvelous to take care of. The Captain's a good mother, and God knows he needed one."

Toni was leaning forward and looking out the door across the street. "My God, look what's coming," she said. Just across the street and starting to cross, there was the Mormon, Captain Marvelous, behind him, poking him in the ribs every couple steps to keep him moving. The Captain was obviously steering him to the door here. Behind the two, padding quietly along, apparently bored but keeping their eyes on the Mormon were three wolves. The Captain shepherded the Mormon through the door, then mildly shoved him to a stool. "Come on, come on. Toni will fix you. She'll have you simply marvelous. Come on, sit down."

The Mormon looked like hell. His face was a bleary blur. His shoes were untied, on over bare feet. One sock stuck out of one of his pants pockets; the other, together with his tie, was stuffed into his shirt pocket. He obediently stumbled against a stool and, concentrating intently, managed to climb on.

"Black coffee for you, baby," Toni said.

"Oh, no, I can't have coffee. I'm a Mormon," he said.

"Something for everybody," Bill Quack yelled out. "On me."

"Got any money, Bill," Toni said.

"Fuck money. I've given you my whole shift. Give everybody something, and don't complain."

Toni refilled Bill and Joe. Captain Marvelous got a screwdriver. Me another Rainier Ale. "Orange juice for you, baby," she said to the Mormon. "Drink up."

"And the wolves. Don't forget the wolves," said Bill. They had come into the bar, squatting in the corner near the door but leaning around enough to keep an eye on the Mormon. Toni found a metal bowl, filled it with draft beer, lifted the flap at the end of the bar, and set the bowl on the floor in front of the wolves. The lead one slurped most of it down, leaving just a little for number two.

"So you took care of him ok, Captain," said Joe.

"And he was not simply marvelous, I must say," said the Captain. "I had to take him back to my place. The poor thing was in no condition. And then he was puking every ten minutes. Thank God the bar is open, and I can put him back where I found him. I don't know why I do all this stuff for you, Joe. You really owe me."

"Because of all the drinks I give you on my shifts, that's why," Joe said. "I've always got you taken care of."

"I don't care. No more Mormon pukers," said the Captain.

Toni was talking to the Mormon. "Drink up." He did, and she poured a second orange juice. "That too. Then you got to get out of here, call home, and figure out how you can get back there. Do you understand that?" Toni had to repeat herself before the Mormon nodded. She made him repeat her instructions. "There's a pay phone across the street. I can't have you keep sitting in my bar. Go on. Go on. Don't be ashamed; just get on with it." The Mormon abstractedly pulled the sock out of his shirt pocket and started to pull off a shoe. "No, no, you can't dress in here. You got to get out now. Stand up. Get out and go make your call. Get up and get out. Now." The Mormon obeyed, slipping off the stool and shambling out the door.

The wolves watched him go, but they weren't really paying attention to him anymore. Instead, they were staring at Toni, the yellow eyes intent, seeming hot and cold at once. You might as well grab Toni as stare at her; she felt it just as palpably. She tried to ignore them for a few moments, but I could see her tail tightening around her torso, squeezing up her tits. And the tail end switched every now and then like a nervous cat. Quickly enough, she'd had it. "OK, the three of you out now. No manners, no service. Out now."

They half stood but moved no further, heads half hung down but still staring intently at her. Bill Quack moved down the bar, waving his arms. "You heard the lady. You've had your drink. Now you're done. Move it, move it, move it." The lead one rose, turned his body toward the door and started out but still staring back over his shoulder at Toni. Bill started quacking at them. The other two followed the leader. Finally, once outside, they turned toward the street, saw the Mormon making his phone call; and padded over and sat down about ten feet away, watching him call.

Bill said to Toni, "Glad to be of service, madam, but when you call for a quack, there's always a bill." And he held out his glass for another. She gave him a half smile and poured.

The Duke strutted in the door, did a little dance shuffle, and said, "Well, now, Toni, Robert told me you was back around, but he didn't tell me you was doing the Limbo Shift. Now, that makes a little more sense. Gives us some better decoration for our drinks."

"What do you want, Duke?"

The Duke raised his eyebrows up and down at her. "Don't play with me, Wiley. I'm not in the mood. I just threw those fucking wolves across the street out of here for staring at me. Don't you be next. What do you want to drink?"

The Duke looked across the street to where the wolves were still watching the Mormon make his phone call. "Them?" he said, "They ain't nothing but street trash. I see them all the time, and they don't do nothing but try to get their courage up. ... Give me a vodka cran."

Toni poured the drink but continued to sulk. She steamed for perhaps ten minutes, then came to a decision. "I've had it. That's enough for a first shift. Bar's closed." Then she brightened a bit. "I've always wanted to do last call at 10 in the morning. It's so decadent. Like déjà vu all over again."

"Last call, folks. Last call for alcohol."

The Duke raised his finger in the air right away; then, when he'd caught Toni's eye, pointed down at his empty glass. Toni poured the drink right over his finger. The Duke shook it dry, at the same time sliding off a nice tip for Toni from his money on the bar.

"That's it," Toni chanted, "Closing time. It's closing time, folks. Drink 'em up right now. Drink 'em up, move 'em out,

Rawhide. Get along, folks. Hotel, motel. I don't care what you do, but you can't do it here. Bar's closed."

This showmanship was just slightly out of character for Toni. She had lots of flair, but, except when she was dancing, used it mostly face to face, not showing off in public. But after all, the few people in the bar right now were all people she'd known years and years: Bill Quack, the Duke, Slick Joe, Captain Marvelous, and me.

"You, baby," she said to me, "I need to wind down a little while. Let me use your apartment, just for a little while, till I can calm down."

"OK," I said. The others had headed off up the street, probably to Gino's. I walked Toni the three blocks or so back to my apartment. "It's easy for the Duke just to call those wolves street trash," she said. "I've been raped by street trash. I thought I was over all that shit when I died." I didn't answer, and she didn't say anything more. When we got inside my apartment, she said, "You just go read or play with your computer or watch a ballgame or something. I just need to be alone a while somewhere safe." She turned away from me, unwound her tail, coiled it on the floor, and used it as a kind of meditation cushion, folding her feet into her lap in the Lotus position and settling herself there. I stood there a moment, then followed her suggestion, went off to my bedroom and turned the TV to a ballgame. An hour later, when I came out to get a glass of water, Toni had gone.

A few days later, I saw Toni in the Saloon talking to Alice Tall. I pulled a stool next to them and listened in. "I need a doorman for the Limbo Shift," Toni was saying, "I want to get hold of Badges."

"Gee, honey," Tall said, "I haven't seen anything of him since he died. Maybe you didn't hear about it? He was going to buy some drugs in Mexico, but it all went bad, and he got shot."

"No, I know about that," Toni said, "but Badges was too strong to just go 'pff' and gone. He'd be great for the Limbo Shift. I just need to find him."

"But Badges died somewhere in Mexico. You don't even know any address or anything."

"I'm still really new at this," Toni said, "but I don't think it's such a problem. It feels like I should be able to put the word out somehow."

"O, sure," I said.

"It's too bad you're not dead. You'd understand a lot better," she said and giggled. "And anyway, it's great being able to stay with you. And you'll find it very educational," she continued, to take any sting out of her words.

"And you, Tall, any help you can give me?"

"Gee, honey, I don't know. But I'll tell Rainier here if I get a line on him. Or you, of course." Tall and Badges had had a kind of relaxed thing going on and off for years.

Badges was not unusually tall – maybe 6 foot one – but he was muscular – and had a kind of sullen lurking ferocity about him. He got his nickname from the time he headed into the Saloon to hear the band, and the new doorman said he needed $5.00 to get in unless he had a stamp on his hand. Badges gave him the old movie line: "Badges? I don't have to show you no stinking badges."

The doorman took a second look at Badges and decided not to make an issue of it.

I remember the first time I saw Badges. I was playing chess at the table in the front window of the Coffee Gallery. (That table later wound up in my apartment as a by-product of the negotiations during an ownership change.) It was a weekend night, so, of course, parking spaces were tight. A big old Oldsmobile made a couple or three circuits looking for a space and finally started trying to pull into a nonspace that wouldn't have held a VW bug. Badges was behind the wheel. He kept trying to saw back and forth to park the Olds until people were streaming out of the bar to watch. "Badges," somebody said, "Whatever it is you're on, have you got any more?"

It turned out it was Alice Small who got the word. Small was maybe the world's champion dumpster diver. She'd go all over the city on her hunts and come up with all kinds of stuff, some valuable, some useful, and some just freakish. She was on one of her Mission District forays and stopped to talk to somebody she knew in a bar out at 14th and Valencia.

There was a story about a local guy who once was making trouble at that bar, got thrown out, and then was busted by a beat cop who happened to be coming by. The cop took him before the judge, and the judge asked, "What are you charging this man with?"

"Disturbing the peace."

"Where did this incident occur?"

"14th and Valencia."

"Case dismissed," the judge said. It was that kind of neighborhood.

Badges had once had a bartending shift at that bar. An intimidating presence was a serious help. But he lost it when one day the owner, who also happened to be a North Beach regular, came into the Coffee Gallery and found Badges drunk there when he should have been tending bar out at 14th and Valencia.

But Badges was a natural working the door. Mostly, once he got to know people, he was fine with them and working the door you soon get to know pretty well the regular people in the neighborhood and the others who hang out now and then. As for neighborhood strangers or troublemakers, that's where the intimidation was an asset. But not the time when, as people were trailing back into the bar after the band had been on break, he stopped one guy and told him, "You got no stamp on your hand. Ten-dollar cover."

"But I'm the bass player."

"Yeah, yeah. Everybody's the bass player. No stamp, ten dollars."

Bill, the owner, saw the confrontation and came over. "Badges, you've got to let him in. He really is the bass player."

Badges needed a long time winding down after that shift. ("Some S.o.B musicians think their shit don't stink.")

Anyhow, Badges used to shoot pool out in the Mission sometimes after hours. Small's friend told her he was still doing it now and then. Small told Tall, Tall told Toni, and the two of them talked to Badges. He said he'd been disoriented right after he died and had just been killing time shooting pool. He said that getting back to North Beach and working the door again would be like coming home.

CHAPTER 3 TONI'S DEATH

Toni had died in my arms. A little over a week before Tall and I had taken her to the doctor to find out whether her cancer had come back. Afterward, she had been in pain, scared, and exhausted by the two or three hours of tests she'd been herded through. I couldn't just take her back to her cheap hotel room down the street – "our little refuge for the criminally insane," as she called it. I had taken her back to my apartment, the same one I'd kicked her out of a couple years before. She lay down on the futon sofa in the front room, not really a comfortable one, but she was too exhausted to care. She only lasted a little more than a week.

But I'm not telling this in order. I need to go back to Toni's mastectomy and how it all developed.

Toni came up to me in the bar in evident distress, took my hand, and put it on her breast to feel her lump. "I have breast cancer," she said. "I have surgery in a couple days." This came to me out of the blue. I'd lost track of Toni after my landlord threw the two of us out of my Romolo Alley apartment. I then deliberately took a studio apartment only big enough for myself. Our life at Romolo had emptied out already before we were thrown out, and I had seen no point in trying to continue it elsewhere.

The way she just came up and automatically put my hand on this private part of her body was very intimate as was her confidence that she could come to me in this awful situation. Toni was terrified of doctors and hospitals. If crisis had not been so long her daily bread, she would have been frantic. At this last minute, she had run out of friends to put her up. I later saw a note her doctor had written to help her apartment hunt. It said that she "is under my care for a life-threatening condition. Please extend whatever accommodation you can to her." No doubt he thought he was helping, but it was careless thinking. A woman in her 50s on SSI with pink, green, blue, and purple hair and a doctor's note saying she has a life-threatening condition is not likely to be high on a landlord's list of desirable tenants.

I remember seeing Toni on the street one day comparing hair with Tweety, the young old lady of one of Toni's biker artist friends. Toni's short, thin hair was then bleached blond with the rainbow shadows of past dyes here and there in undertones. I used to say that any woman's hair color was just like Toni's, no matter what the color, if you just picked the right time. For a long time, it had been a dark brick red, but sometimes fire engine, and at one time or another, any color you can think of. Tweety's hair was some bright color, all frizzed out in a halo round her head, and Tweety wore black lipstick, a bright tank top, and lots of beads. She was almost as skinny as Toni and towered over her a good ten inches. In all unconscious sincerity, she was saying to Toni, "No, Toni, I couldn't be as radical as you. You're just too much."

Tweety was right. As with Hamlet, so with Toni: "These things indeed seem, for these are the actions that a man might play. But I have that within which passeth show; these but the trappings and the suits of outrageousness."

Tweety had told Toni one time about wanting to get her old man some art supplies for his birthday. "You know, one of those pentagrams he uses to draw with."

"You mean a Pentel?"

"Yeah, like I said."

Another time, one of Tweety's friends came up and interrupted while Toni and Tweety were talking. "Wow. Guess what I'm living with now," the friend said to Tweety.

"What?" Tweety said.

"A classical pianist!"

"A classical penis?" Toni asked innocently. "Can he play 'Roll me over/In the clover/ Roll me over, lay me down, and do it again."

Tweety and her friends just looked puzzled.

Toni left them to their gossip, came over to me, and said, "What rooty-poots."

Back to Toni and her cancer. I called good friends of mine who knew Toni slightly and described Toni's predicament, indirectly sounding them as to whether they might put Toni up for a couple nights. Clearly no interest there. I ended up taking Toni back to my little studio where we talked together and shared my twin bed like brother and sister.

Toni's anxiety notwithstanding, the surgery itself went by uneventfully and with a moderately hopeful prognosis, though she would need follow-up chemotherapy. The real problem was finding a place for her to stay. Tall put her up for a short while right out of the hospital, but it was hard because the Alice hadn't much space, and Toni and Small didn't really get along. I told Toni I would share a place with her again, but, of course, it would take a little time to find one. In the end it was Crystal who came through.

Crystal Ball was a young topless dancer with a gorgeous figure and a squeaky voice. She'd arrived in North Beach under age as Dorothy Potts. Guys were always ready to buy her drinks, so the bars didn't think to ask for her ID. She told me once that when she got to North Beach, "I wanted to be completely independent and find somebody to take care of me." She'd gotten a cheap hotel room, and she said one time she'd thought a guy cute who came into the bar with a "Deaf and Dumb, Please Help" card. She took him back to her room and screwed him. A couple days later, there was a pounding on her door. "Who is it?" she squeaked. More pounding. "Who is it? I'm not letting anybody in unless I know who." More pounding, more "Who is it?" Finally, a deaf and dumb card slid under the door.

A couple times, Toni had brought Crystal back to the Romolo apartment as a brief refuge when she was fighting with the biker boyfriend she'd hooked up with. (This guy really was fond of Crystal and, in his own way, had a good heart. After one of these occasions, he came up to me as I was walking down the alley. He was a big guy, and I was nervous about what was going to happen. But he said, "I just want to tell you how I appreciate you and Toni taking care of Crystal. If there's ever anything I can do for you – for example, beat somebody up – just let me know." Whew.) Crystal told me once that she and her biker liked to shoot pool for who would be on top. "But," she said, "it really doesn't make any difference. It all works out the same anyway."

The biker was history by now, and Crystal was living with Arthur, a guy in his 50s who owned a bar out in the Mission. "It's got to be Arthur, not Art:", he tells everybody, because if they call him Art, he thinks they will think he's Arturo, and he's not, he's Arthur. When she got mad at him, Crystal called him, "Arturo, Arturo, Arturo." He was furious and told Crystal never never to call him that again. "So I call him, 'Tora! Tora! Tora!' He knows what I mean."

Crystal told him, "Toni has to have a place to go for a little while. We have to put her up till she can find a place." And Arthur went along with it. But Crystal and Arthur didn't last that long. Arthur had enough sense not to expect Crystal just to settle down with him; nevertheless, that was really what he wanted. She'd be gone for a day or two, Arthur would sulk then quarrel, and Crystal would squeak, "Tora! Tora! Tora!" Crystal couldn't take it anymore and finally wouldn't go back. Toni, of course, had to go too.

I saw Crystal in the Saloon a little later scheming how to get back a lot of her stuff still in Arthur's apartment. She was enlisting Frankie, a big no-account guy – maybe 30 or so -- from a wealthy family whose parents sent him a check every month to keep him away from home. The check would run out by the middle of the month, forcing him to sober up for a while until the next check arrived. He'd show up sober the first of the month looking almost like a rising executive and start his slide to a broke mid-month.

One time, Crystal told me she came back from a trip, arriving late at night just in time to make last call at the Saloon. It was already nearly a week into the new month, and nobody had seen Frankie. There were rumors going around that he was dead. Crystal, having gotten a little heat on, decided she should be a Good Samaritan. It just so happened that somehow, she had Frankie's mother's phone number. She called Mom back in Texas at about 3:30 AM:

"Ms. Jefferson, this is Crystal. You don't know me, but I'm Frankie's friend. Now, I just got back in town so I don't know everything, and I don't want to alarm you, but Frankie may be dead."

"Well, Crystal, thank you for calling. Were you able to check the jail?"

"No."

"How about the General Hospital?"

"No."

"Did you check the morgue?"

"No."

"Well, Crystal, I would appreciate it if you could check like that and call me back."

Crystal slept. In the morning, she thought she'd first check by Frankie's apartment. Frankie didn't answer the bell, but the manager knew her and let her into Frankie's place. She found him collapsed on his bed on the bad end of a 6-day run. She got him conscious with lots of black coffee.

"Now, Frankie," she said, "I don't want to get into a lot of stuff with you, but you better call home."

Now at the Saloon, she'd bought Frankie a couple drinks, promised him more afterward, and explained what she wanted him to do. She had a cab driver friend who would take them to Arthur's apartment. "You stand there and yell at him while Sandy and I get my stuff out." Apparently, it worked because later in the day, I saw Crystal buying Frankie the rest of his drinks.

Toni and I had talked with Grace about finding an apartment together. Grace was our former across-the-hall neighbor at

Romolo. Grace was a copier technician who moonlighted as a psychic. Her daughter Lily had just recently moved out on her own, and Grace agreed to look for a new place to share with Toni and me. We had already found some prospects when Arthur threw Toni out. Grace took Toni into her apartment for the short time necessary to complete arrangements.

Toni had befriended Lily shortly after Grace moved into Romolo. Lily was only eleven or so at the time and was fascinated by Toni. Toni would let her visit while she worked away at a collage or mask or whatever, and Lily would ask her questions about growing up, boys, and sex. Toni mostly evaded them.

"Don't ask me," Toni said one time, "I'm a dinosaur."

"What kind of dinosaur," little Lily teased.

"Terribillismis Christmas Kissimus. Now go home, and let me concentrate on my work."

Little Lily once gave Toni a gift to seal their friendship: her training bra. "It's too small for me," she told Toni. Toni managed not to laugh as she accepted it.

Toni, Grace, and I settled on a two-bedroom place on Broadway on the top floor with a little convenience store on the street level. Grace and I each took a bedroom, and Toni, for a lesser rent, slept in the front room. I was out of town when Toni and Grace moved in, only arriving back a couple weeks into the month. The place had high ceilings, and Toni had gotten a carpenter friend of hers to build her a little loft in the front room, something the landlord was not in the least happy about when he discovered it. Still, he put up with it.

But it wasn't working out. Toni wasn't getting follow-up chemotherapy and wasn't even seeing the doctor. She wasn't paying her reduced rent. She and I each went about our business and had little to say to one another. Then, one night, I was wakened by sounds from Toni's little loft. She was screwing a young guy she'd recently met in the bars. I would have tolerated the no medical care, no rent, little talk situation, but damned if I was going to have her bringing somebody back to screw in my apartment.

I saw a lawyer who told me I couldn't just lock her out. If necessary, I could evict her. His suggestion: "Give her some money to get a new place. That's the most practical way to work it."

I spoke to Grace and asked her whether she was happy with the situation in the apartment. Grace said no. She'd recently hooked up with a new man. Toni didn't approve of him and didn't want him in the apartment. Grace now wanted to replace Toni with her new man.

I talked to Toni. "You can't stay here this way any longer. You've got to go. You're not paying the rent you agreed. I took this with you so you could get follow-up chemo, and you haven't even seen the doctor since the surgery. I give you until the end of the month to find a new place, and I'll pay the first month's rent for you – within reason. If you're not out by then, I'll evict you, and I won't help you with anything.". I didn't say anything about the guy she screwed. It wasn't a good conversation – how could it possibly be? -- but it wasn't awful. I guess Toni was used to being thrown out of places by then. She found a room in a cheap hotel a few doors down Broadway from us.

After a month or two I started visiting Toni in her "little refuge." I can't recall quite how it started. It was a small room. Even though I was storing a lot of Toni's stuff for her – including a lot of her artwork on my walls – her cheap hotel room here was still packed with miscellaneous possessions, stuff she'd acquired, art she was working on, and stuff she thought she might work on. She had become a kind of den mother. She told me about a guy there with a twisted sexual relationship, full of passion, jealousy, and fucked up affection. She had a piece of artwork he'd created. Cutouts from photos of the head and torso of each of them angled together from the bottom to form a sort of heart. He'd put a nail through the heart at the bottom where the two torsos came together, then spilled his own blood over it and smeared it into another heart shape. Of course, the original crimson had dried and left a brown, cracking and flaking crust. It was a disturbing piece from a disturbed person.

Toni was great with people like this who were even more inwardly vulnerable than she. She would listen, argue, give advice, and sympathize, but without really expecting her arguments to be listened to, her advice taken, or her sympathy to make much difference. And yet it did. It didn't cure, but it was solace. Some of the people she mothered this way would grow past their troubles, others not, and who could tell which would be which. But regardless, a little solace is good, isn't it?

Others there were less sympathetic. Toni talked about a girl who visited her sometimes. "I have to watch her close so she can't steal anything. Most people who steal from you feel guilty about it and then hold it against you. But she doesn't. If I catch her, she just puts it back and goes right on talking, hoping I'll get distracted and she'll get something then." Toni would warn me about the people here, just as through all the years I knew her, she did about the people she talked to in the bars and on the street. "Just because I talk to them, it doesn't mean they're alright. It doesn't mean you should talk to them. You have to be careful." It takes a tough life to develop instinctive street smarts like Toni's.

From time to time, when she wasn't feeling well, Toni would phone me and ask me to pick things up for her. It always included cigarettes. It grated on me to get them for her – no medical care and still puffing away regular as a factory. (It reminded me of when I was a kid in Cleveland hearing about the time the Cuyahoga River became so polluted it caught on fire.) Nevertheless, I knew it was pointless to argue with her about smoking, and I got them for her. Then she called me like this about two years after I'd kicked her out of the Broadway apartment. When I delivered her supplies, she was in bed in pain. She said she'd been that way a couple days now and had scarcely had anything to eat in that time. I talked with her for a while, finally leaving in some concern. I checked in with her again the next day to see if she'd improved. Still in pain, still very weak, still not eating. "Toni," I told her, "You've got to see the doctor, if only to get some pain relief." She was too weak to argue.

The fear that her cancer was reasserting itself was naturally in my mind, as it surely was also in Toni's. I looked up hospices in San Francisco, called the medical director of one of them, and made an appointment for him to see Toni. Tall drove us there. Ordinarily, I would never get in a car with Tall driving, but, in the circumstances, it was nothing. Tall and I waited while Toni went in for her exam then while she was sent from station to station for tests and more tests. She went from one to another very docilely like a good girl. It was something like three hours before they were

through with her. I took Toni back to the Broadway apartment –
Grace and her man had moved out a little while before, and I was
alone there. I couldn't just dump Toni back in her hotel room. She
had at least gotten something for her pain. She lay down on an
uncomfortable futon sofa in the living room. She was too
exhausted to be particular. Before she conked out, she had
something urgent to tell me. "Back at the doctor's," she said, "That
wasn't me. I didn't want to let them push me around, but I was just
too weak and scared and hurt too much. But that wasn't really me."

The doctor phoned me the next morning early. Toni was still
conked out. "I don't know yet whether her cancer is back or not.
She's got a lump in her belly I can feel, but I won't know until a
few days when the biopsy gets back if it's cancer. But her kidneys
have shut down. She'll die from that if she's not admitted to the
hospital right away for acute hemodialysis. Ordinarily, I would just
order an ambulance for her, but since you came to me through the
Hospice, I'm making this call to ask you what you want to do." I
told him Toni was sleeping and I would have to call him back.

I went out to the bars to see if I could find some of Toni's
friends to talk to. I talked a little to Tall and to a couple other of
her friends. Each of them was sympathetic and distressed, but none
of them wanted to give any advice. There really weren't a lot of
choices to weigh.

I went back to Toni, woke her, and told her what the doctor
had told me. She was only half conscious but wasn't in any doubt
about what she wanted. "No hospital," she said. I called the doctor
and told him Toni's decision. He started the wheels right away to
enroll Toni in hospice care in my apartment. I thought then and
still think Toni made the right decision. Regardless of whether her
cancer had come back, I think her health was pretty much wrecked,

particularly considering how she lived her life. In the days that followed, she never showed any second thoughts.

The Hospice people set up a hospital bed in my empty bedroom the next day. Toni showed no interest in it. They also found a Home Health Aide to come in during the day. Earlier there had been a big layoff at work, and, with my many years there, I had gotten a fat layoff check. I'd been using it to take a kind of sabbatical and had enrolled in some multi-media classes at San Francisco State. The idea was that the Home Health Aid could look after Toni while I was in class. She turned out to be a Russian woman, well-meaning but fussy and managing. The mess in the apartment distressed her. Even worse, in her eyes, Toni was not eating. When I got home that first day, she lectured me about the mess. "It's really not my job, but I did clean up some of it for you, but it's not my job. And I tried to get her to eat, but she won't eat. You have to get her to eat."

"Thank you very much," I told her. "But I find I will be able to stay home and take care of her. It won't be necessary for you to come in anymore." The aide fussed and sputtered a bit, but I was very clear to her that I appreciated her coming today but would not need her help anymore.

Toni's problem was not getting something to eat or apartment mess. The main problem she had was that the initial medications the hospice provided had her twitching every now and again. That night, I got out of bed to go to the john and found Toni standing in a kind of sleepwalking state in the hall. I put my hands on her shoulders, turned her around, and started steering her from behind to lie down again. As I did so, I leaned forward and kissed her on the back of the neck. She perked up enough to tease me about it. "Watch it, buster," she said.

"I love you, Toni," I said.

"I love you too, baby," she said, just a little above a whisper.

I am so glad we got those words in. Notwithstanding, I feel sure had Toni somehow magically recovered, our life with one another would have been full of frustrations, just as it had been all along. Our connection had been like a top that should be spinning down but instead just wobbles all over the place, then straightens up as if everything is fine then off wobbling again. But what actually happens is not all of reality. Sometimes, it is lit from within like a kind of magic lantern and light show. It is having this kind of power switch at hand that makes the other stuff trivial.

Lots of closeness is indirect. I think of talking with Toni not long after she had first moved in with me at Romolo Alley. There was a parking lot outside, and at night, the headlights from the cars going through the alley and in the lot cast moving shadows through the bamboo shades on my windows onto the walls. I can't recall what we were saying – nothing in particular – but in the middle of it, Toni said, in a casual kind of way, "I'm hallucinating now." It was the hypnotic effect of those shadow puppets on the walls. And I learned something else in that conversation: I would see things like that simply as flat patterns on the wall. Toni saw three-dimensional shapes, like the forms you can see in cloud stacks.

This sort of trick of vision showed up surprisingly in one of her paintings, an acrylic about three and a half feet by two and a half. When I first looked at it, I saw a man's face floating in space. It was the face only, no skull, rendered rather like M. C. Escher's print, "Rinds," with the face in a spiral like an apple paring. I said something about the face to her and discovered that, until then, she had not seen it at all. Instead, she had painted a brazen female nude of the kind you might see on velvet hanging in a bar. I then saw the nude she'd painted while she discovered the man's face I had first seen. It was one of those things where the image you see clicks back and forth.

"I didn't know the man was there," she said, "but at the same time, I must have because I painted him." To me, neither one in itself was outstanding, but the way they cohabited in the exact same space was.

The next morning, I talked to the doctor about Toni twitching in her sleep, and he added something for it– Valium, I think it was. In any case, I was able to get it during the day, and it did take care of the twitching. Toni drifted peacefully in and out of consciousness over the next few days. During the years Toni had lived with me, I saw her sleeping routinely, and she was not a peaceful sleeper. That made me the more grateful for her peacefulness these last days, and I did not attribute it only to the drugs.

The next day, a social worker came to do the paperwork to enroll Toni in the hospice. She was young, pleasant, and sincere. Toni answered some of the questions and I the rest as Toni's focus drifted in and out.

"Do you live here?" the social worker asked, her pen poised over her form.

Toni, bless her heart, smiled and started a sort of meditative reminiscence of the whole story of how she had first moved in with me on Romolo and seemed ready to tell the whole story of our ups and downs from place to place. Her obliviousness to the practical situation now and absorption in the inwardness of how we had lived together touched me.

However, I caught her first long pause to interrupt. "Yes, you can put down she lives here."

I wanted the social worker to appreciate something of who Toni was, so I said, "Toni is an artist," and pointed out some of her things on the apartment walls. The social worker made some sort of sympathetic and appreciative remark. "And she was an excellent dancer," I said.

The social worker perked up a little. "Really? Ballet? Or modern dance?" I couldn't resist the opening. "No," I said, "A stripper."

To tell the truth, I don't really know whether Toni was ever a stripper or not. She might well have been. I just knew her as a dancer from the bars and knew she truly put body and soul into it.

I had, as I say, been touched by how Toni started to tell our history to the social worker. It showed that it had been on her mind and, more than that, that she placed great value on it. Over the next day or so, I spent a lot of time thinking about it myself, analyzing it, and rehearsing explanations of it from my point of view to present to Toni. In fact, I never delivered them. Toni was never awake enough for that sort of conversation, and maybe that was a blessing.

To tell the truth, I don't really believe things are solved within intimate relationships by intricate rational analysis by the parties to it. O, I will do it in my head, to be sure, and even think all that going over it has some use in orienting me. But the basic things take place at geologic levels, like the joining or sundering of tectonic plates and where what is visible at the surface is incidental to those deep forces. You need nerve ends reaching way down to sense what's basic.

We got the "I love you" exchange in in the nick of time. A day or two later, she died, as I have told you. A woman from the hospice came out, a very sensitive one. She asked me whether it was ok for her to wash her body, and that it was something that she liked to do. I said, "Yes, ok." She did so, and afterward, Toni lay there looking clean and composed. "She farted at me while I was cleaning her," the woman said. "God, it was a big one for such a little woman. That doesn't often happen." But that was Toni, the imp, the trouble-maker. I was glad to hear (but not to smell) that she had recovered the courage that had failed her when Tall and I had taken her to the doctor.

I took a photo of Toni lying in bed after the hospice woman had washed her. Some people were uncomfortable that I had taken her picture that way, but it is one I'm very glad to have. It touched my heart. As I say, she looked clean and composed. But also, all the outrageousness had disappeared. It was just a little aging woman who looked reconciled to both existence and nonexistence.

"Sorrow is better than laughter. for by the sadness of the countenance the heart is made better." (Ecclesiastes 7:3). Knowing sorrow, we know that this is not the best of all possible worlds. The heart cannot but know regret even without knowing exactly what for. It is in the nature of the heart beat. We can neither fully accept nor reject the world as it is. Those who know no sorrow know no hope. Toni had wrestled with both as Jacob did with the angel."

There was a memorial for her a few days later at Specs. Just a few people, one table was enough. I brought three of her smaller pieces to it and some of my poems about her were glued onto cardboard to make a poster. Tall was there. Marlene was there also. I had met her only after Toni died, but she'd been a good friend to

Toni. Toni had used Marlene's address to get her SSI check.
Having her check addressed to her "little refuge for the criminally
insane" wouldn't have been safe. When I had met Marlene a day or
two before, she and I had talked some about Toni, and Marlene had
told me a little about her own life. She had, she said, married a
high school sweetheart and had a son with him. Then, she fell into
a passionate affair with her husband's best friend. It caused a
divorce, and the affair had not ended well. She had withstood it all.
During this talk, I knew her only as Marlene, but before the
memorial I chanced to see the envelope to one of Toni's SSI
checks with the c/o address on it. Seeing Marlene's last name, the
name of her ex that she was still using, I realized with a jolt that I
knew both her ex and her son. The ex was a cab driver, a man at
once cynical and sweet-tempered, and a good friend of Firebird's.
The son seemed so innocent and straight that it seemed improbable
that he should hang out in North Beach. We told stories about Toni
and her tangled life. It wasn't that Toni hadn't planned. She always
had lots of plans, and she put her heart into all of them –
everything wholeheartedly but with a divided heart. As we talked
at Specs, in the flow of conversation, Marlene popped out with
Toni's eulogy, marvelously succinct: "If you knew Toni, you
really loved her, and you wanted to kill her."

CHAPTER 4 RHYTHM OF THIS STORY

I like murder mysteries myself. First, they set the scene; then there's a murder, then lots of false trails and confusion; finally, everything is straightened out at the end. It's a classic form of storytelling. Start at the beginning, go to the end, and then stop. But it's artificial. Life is always in the middle, looking both backward and forwards. In practice, we never get to read the last chapter. It is in the nature of life, even of reality itself, that nothing gets finally cleared up -- not past nor present, nor future. What I think is that our vision exists in a tension with confusion on the one hand and with reality on the other. A vision completely realized is dead. Living vision is an intuition that contains more than is directly seen. Like an iceberg, two-thirds is underneath. And confusion tells us that visions, even when they seem very clear, still don't get the whole picture just right.

This is like one of those trees that have all kinds of fruit growing on it – part story, a part reminiscence and part meditation -- sometimes serious, sometimes casual – such as might take place over several sessions, perhaps in one of my North Beach bars, as we got to know one another, and I tell you about both the important and casual things in my life. Each of the two adds dimension and questions to the other.

Or this is like one of Toni's collages. She always built them from intuition, from trying out different combinations of things from the boxes of magazine pictures and other photos she had – never from logic. They made a strong impression but a mixed one that you couldn't explain all at once. It's kind of like I have a box full of the people, places, and scenes of North Beach to reach into. Toni and I, and the Limbo Shift are the big bits in this collage, but there's a lot of the rest of that world scrambled in. All the background and the foreground affected me all at once, and this is my intuition of them.

Frederick Douglass, the great black abolitionist, wrote about how hearing the moaning songs of slaves working in the fields inexpressibly moved him. William Loyd Garrison, the great white abolitionist, praised Douglass for a poem Douglass wrote about how the brooks and rivers run free to the sea, but he cannot be free. Garrison thought that the poem showed how a black man could be capable of higher things. To me, that poem, as Garrison described it, seemed a very conventional one. That high culture seemed to me rather like plastic flowers. North Beach seemed to me like the slave songs. moving me not directly but from the context. Those songs were not exactly songs without words, and the sound wasn't exactly musical. What so moves you is somehow jumbled up with words and sounds but inexpressible. It is a song heard not so much with the ears as with the bones.

I talk about a lot of people and bars in North Beach. They are a sort of extended family us regulars. No doubt it's hard to take this in all at once, so don't try. If you really get too puzzled at some points, I've put an Appendix at the end about the bars and people of North Beach. But don't try to get all the details straight. In my opinion, that's a good way not to get the feel of the place. And if you find it confusing, then you've got the feel of the place.

CHAPTER 5 ME

It's time you got to know me a little more.

Growing up and until I went to Mississippi, I imagined I would become a somewhat unconventional person with a successful career. Then, becoming a civil rights volunteer in the1964 Mississippi Summer Project changed my life. I came out wanting to change the world but got stalled as to how it could be done. In 1970, I came to San Francisco to visit college friends before refusing the Vietnam draft. I was full of confusion about my direction in life; and all unexpectedly, my fate led me into the bars of North Beach.

Growing Up

Each of my parents came from small conservative towns -- my father in Indiana and my mother in Florida. They met in a small central Florida college during the Depression.. They came out of it liberals amidst conservatives. My father's mother was very disappointed in him that he had left a job at Marshall Field's department store in Chicago to go to college in Florida. He wound up a social worker.

When I was a five-year-old, there was a little girl next door who used to read me my favorite books. She was maybe in first or second grade. I had those books memorized, and I used to prompt her when she was having trouble with words. It sort of set an expectation in me that I would be able to know better like that all my life. When I was a kid, maybe ten or eleven, I remember my father bringing someone he'd met at work home for dinner. Afterwards they were talking, and the guest said something about how the accidents of life, not any plan, had landed him in his career. My father made no particular comment, but I could see his sympathy. I was too well-trained to say anything, but I was a little shocked. You were supposed to study life, come to a purposeful decision, then steadfastly carry it out. That was what life was all about — or would or should be — that was how I saw it. My fate, reading my mind over my shoulder, must have chuckled.

Later, when I was a teenager, and my father was a case work supervisor for a United Way agency that worked with delinquent teens, my father told a story about a Polish teen, I think it was, who had thrown his grandmother out the window. It was a ground-floor window, and Grandma was more outraged than hurt. My father wasn't outraged. He seemed to find the story an example of family vitality. Who knows? Sometimes, outrageous incidents like that can kind of clear the air for healing. Sometimes, it just exacerbates things. I enjoyed the story though it was from a different world from mine. Somehow, I seemed to have inherited my father's love for disorderly vitality. To be sure, it plays the imp with straightforward purposefulness, but perhaps it was North Beach beckoning.

When it came time for college, I was so proud to get into the College at the University of Chicago, a school at once prestigious, intellectual, and, as I saw it, unconventional. Being on my own there was a heady, liberating experience. I was delighted orienting myself in the great world, making friends, having ideas, and vaguely moving toward some sort of fulfilling, challenging career. Civil rights direct action had sprung up around the country in the 60's. In the great big1963 March on Washington I marched and stood in front of the Lincoln Memorial listening to the speeches. Next year, becoming a civil rights volunteer in the 1964

Mississippi Freedom Summer seemed an altogether natural thing to do,

Mississippi and Activism

If I'd never gone to Mississippi, I don't think I'd ever have wound up deep in the bars of North Beach. Mississippi was more than I bargained for. There were a few hundred of us volunteers, mainly white northern college students. We were to go to Mississippi for the summer to register voters, run Freedom Schools, and see whether there were federal programs that might ease the poverty of poor black folks. Before the volunteer training in Oxford, Ohio, was even over three workers – two white, one black – disappeared in Neshoba County, Mississippi. The whites were a guy who had already been organizing in Mississippi and a college volunteer who had arrived in Mississippi only a few days ago as part of the first group to come down. The black guy was a young Mississippian who had joined the Movement. Their murdered bodies were found under a dam much later, but the Movement was sure from the time they disappeared that they were dead. I recall Jimmy Travis, a black Mississippi organizer just slightly older than me, speaking at a meeting with volunteers like me who were still in training. "It's hell in Mississippi," he kept repeating. He himself had been shot in the neck and nearly killed by Mississippi whites a year or so ago. We volunteers were suddenly confronted with what our summer could be like, and it scared us shitless.

I ended up in Canton, a small town not far from Jackson, the state capital. No life and death confrontations for me, but it was still an awakening. I was teaching in a Freedom School with two female volunteers in a little church. The church was right next to what had been a saw mill town, but the saw mill had burned long ago, leaving just the shacks where the workers had lived. The kids from these, small kids to high school age, came to the Freedom School. We taught a mix of things. Some of the teen age guys wanted to learn to write better so they could compose hot bragging letters to attractive girls. One day, an old white man drove up to where a knot of us were sitting outside. One of the female volunteers was sitting with a small black boy on her lap, and a black teenage boy was talking to her. The white man got out of his car, waving a big hoe handle at us. He was shaking, barely in control of himself. He gestured at the volunteer, and said, trembling, "Dew yew call yoreself white?" He repeated it a couple times. We just stood our ground and didn't say much. At length he ran out of steam, said something else nasty, got back in his car, and drove off. Thank God for anti-climaxes. We learned the old man collected the rents from the shacks. He liked to brandish that hoe handle at the residents and got away with it because nasty white folks could do more or less what they wanted with blacks in 1964 Mississippi.

By the end of the summer, there had been a lot of national publicity and a lot of local dramas; but, for me, what mainly happened was it became plain to me how far both Mississippi and the nation were from the world Martin Luther King dreamed about. In the Movement, people – the same people – were regularly saying two things: "We must have Freedom Now" and "I don't expect to see the change in my lifetime." Inconsistent, to be sure, but neither the goal nor the reality could be ignored. I decided to stay in Mississippi after the summer rather than return to college.

After the summer, I joined a project in West Point in northeast Mississippi. It was a pressure cooker, not simply because of background threats to our safety or the strains of organizing under them, but also because of the indirect pressure on ordinary human relations. A black woman on disability living with her 12-year-old son put up three of us in her 4-room tin-top house. Running water only from a fixture outside. There was our Project Manager Ike, a dark-skinned black guy from Chicago who had grown up outside Atlanta; Ernie, a young black street guy from Chicago; and me. Ike told stories about how his daddy had made his way into the black middle class by making whiskey and how, though a Deacon in the church, his daddy had put nothing in the collection plate for six months after the Reverend preached a sermon against liquor. He also talked about how the Atlanta NAACP had wanted to start school integration with light-skinned kids in the name of gradualism. One time, a young white woman, a volunteer from Dartmouth, had surprised Ike naked taking a bath in a tin tub in the bedroom where she had put some clothes. "Ah-ah-o-oh," she gasped. "What's the matter?" Ike asked, "You never seen a nigger's black ass before?"

In the summer of '65, there were big demonstrations in Jackson, the state Capital. They arrested hundreds and put us in livestock barns at the state fairgrounds, tended by game wardens – white demonstrators on one side of the barn, black on the other. We were there for about three days altogether. Somebody, no doubt one of the wardens, dumped a bunch of salt in the breakfast grits, making them inedible. A white liberal Jackson resident came to express his sympathy, but his nervousness at what he was doing spoiled the intended effect. He warned us, all with two-day beards, "Just a word to you, fellas. Beards are not in this year." He asked whether there was anything he could do for us. Somebody asked him to bring some playing cards. "O, I can't come back here," he said.

We went to Washington, DC for some lobbying in the fall. I was burnt out by then. Coming back, we went through Chapel Hill, North Carolina. I had a courtesy aunt there, an old friend of my parents who had moved back to her native home and who had often urged me to visit her. When I showed up without warning, she was very happy to see me, but a few days after showing up, I attended an anti-Vietnam War meeting on the University of North Carolina campus. A perfectly tame event to me. But not to Aunt Marge. Her voice trembled as she asked me, "Robert, did you come here to visit me, or were you sent?" It reminded me of the Christmas card I'd gotten in Mississippi from my grandmother in Jacksonville, Florida, obliquely tolerating my wayward civil rights trouble-making: "Robert, this is just to tell you that I love you anyway." I told Aunt Marge, "I'll find another place fast." And I did – rooming with some of the students from the Vietnam demonstration.

Pretty soon, I had a temporary job filling out socio-economic survey coding sheets for computer data entry. I got a ride to the job from my supervisor, a grad student in something or other for whom this was also a fill-in job. The other car pooler was the young and rather attractive pregnant wife of another grad student. One morning, she started crying, telling the story of her awful experience during a maternity exam at the university hospital. Somehow, she had accidentally gotten into the clinic for welfare mothers, and the resident examining her had made suggestive cracks about who the father might be. She said, "It's a shame to think they treat welfare patients that way, … but I guess they have to be professional." "Professional, like shit," I thought. But our supervisor nodded to her. I kept my mouth shut.

I had caught my breath in Chapel Hill and, when the temporary job was over, went on to Newark, where Tom Hayden was leading an organizing project in the black ghetto. I wanted to join up, but they didn't need more. One of the locals they had enlisted in their project was TJ, a heavy drinker and a charming man who knew everybody. He told me a story. White coeds who volunteered to organize in the ghetto often had a big problem with how to respond to black teens who wanted to hit on a white woman. One white girl who had been there long enough to adapt asked TJ to speak to a recently joined white girl having this kind of problem.

TJ told me, "I sat down next to her when she was alone in the front room of the project apartment. I asked her, 'Well, how do you like the project?' "

"O, I think the project is wonderful," she said.

"Well, how do you like the people in the community?"

"O, I think the people in the community are wonderful."

"Well, how do you like me?"

"O, I think you're wonderful?"

"Want to fuck?"

"O, I think that would be wonderful."

"Listen, I want to explain something: the people in this community have been fucked before. You're here to organize them politically."

"What's the matter? Am I too skinny?"

Though they didn't need volunteers in Newark, they put me in touch with Father Tower, a white Episcopal priest in Jersey City who was organizing rent strikes in the black ghetto. He was a man in his thirties, perhaps, in a big old church that had long ago been full up with white parishioners but for a long time now had been a half-full black church. He had an intense social conscience and signed me up to help with his organizing. The pressure he lived under reminded me of Mississippi. Father Tower had a nervous tic that kept him blinking his eyes constantly. I got a job as a breakfast cook in a YWCA cafeteria and, in my off hours, canvassed for rent strikes together with Jacob, a young black guy Father Tower had helped with delinquency dilemmas and then recruited to help organize.

I had a different education in the realities of the local situation than the girl in Newark. I had just turned 21 and was delighted to be able now to drink legally. I saw a black bar, walked in, sat down on a stool, ordered a beer, and waited a bit uncertainly, wanting to find a way to strike up a conversation with the guy next to me and turn him on to his true political consciousness. I hadn't thought of anything, and then, seeing my beer empty, the guy offered to buy me another. "Far out," I said to myself, readying my spiel. The new beer had scarcely appeared before I felt the guy's heel coming down on my instep. "What are you doing?" I said.

"Well, I bought you a drink, didn't I?" he said.

"I think I'm in the wrong bar," I said and left fast. It was too clear then who was awakening who.

On one occasion, I went over to Newark to join a demonstration there, part of International Days of Protest against the Vietnam war. A young black woman gave a good speech (reminiscent of the things Muhammed Ali was saying at the time) about how the Vietnam War was not in the interests of the poor people of Vietnam nor in the interests of the poor people being drafted to fight it. Afterward, an old black woman in a cloth coat and cotton stockings came up to the girl and got in her face, repeating over and over, "Child, you better watch what you say. The black man can't give you nothing. The white man give you everything you got." The girl tried to walk away, but the old woman kept following her, repeating her litany. Finally, the girl turned on her, "Get away from me old woman. The black man at least can give you a black eye."

Pretty soon, I had my own problems with the draft. I had had a deferment because of unresolved arrests during demonstrations in Mississippi. Finally, though, these were settled, and my deferment was disappearing. I had to get back in college and was able to work that out with my parents and the school. The rent strikes were still up in the air. I hadn't been terrible in working on them but better at hanging out with the people than organizing them. I don't think I was a great loss.

Back in school in Chicago, my life divided among classes toward a Bachelor's degree, anti-Vietnam War activity, and personal relationships. The first two intertwined as anti-Vietnam events came on campus. As for personal relationships, I became close to two artists, Sarah and John. Sarah had been in the University of Chicago College, and I was introduced by friends. She had dropped out and gone briefly to a state school in southern Illinois, where she met John. Both were too much absorbed in their creative vision – both loved Art Nouveaux – to pay much attention to anything else. Sarah and John had dropped out and come to Chicago to find jobs while they oriented their lives. I remember

John telling me about wanting to study a painting he was looking at in the Chicago Art Institute. There were no chairs or benches nearby, and he went looking for one. At length he found a chair in another gallery and was carrying it back to study the painting that interested him. A guard stopped him. It was a Louis XIVth chair he'd picked up from a furniture exhibition.

I used to make long speeches to them about the need to relate one's life to what was happening in the great world, but, in fact, their artistic self-absorption became a kind of refuge for my confusion about activism and study.

In truth, I was a fish out of water. Neither the complacent mainstream nor the militant visions of transformation seemed to me in touch with reality. A militant former student who had been drafted spoke to a rally about why he was accepting induction: "We on the left need to learn how to use guns." Pure frustration, though I understood the sentiment.

I attended a large meeting where a Progressive Labor speaker talked about how he had become a machinist at International Harvester to organize the working class. The black caucus in the union had wanted to lower the requirements to become a machinist. This organizer spoke out, saying, "I could teach anyone to become a machinist in two weeks." He was elected an honorary member of the black caucus but almost lynched by his fellow white machinists. "Actually," he said, "I exaggerated, but the black caucus was the revolutionary element."

At the same meeting, a young woman spoke about how she thought it unfair to say that the working class had sold out on the war in Vietnam. As she spoke, it was evident that the working class existed for her as a real personality, almost as if it were an uncle of hers. The sellout charges were a direct insult to family. The working class hadn't that personal immediacy for me, nor did I much share her confidence that it really was opposed to the Vietnam War. But the ideas the "practical, realistic" mainstream expressing seemed to me no less colored by wishes than hers, and she had more heart. I recalled hearing a faculty member talking indulgently to a group of students, "It's very natural that you should have radical ideas at this time in your life; but once you have real responsibilities like a mortgage, things will be different." Another professor speaking at a Vietnam panel discussion gave his time to talk about how the mission of the university was to seek truth, not to involve itself in politics. When a student asked about some extreme statements by faculty members about what should be done with student demonstrators, the professor shrugged it off: "O, don't pay much attention to those. We were all too angry to think rationally at the time."

Everywhere, slogans and dogma. None of the kind of life awakening among the community and among organizers that had stirred me so in Mississippi and changed the direction of my life. Jersey City had been more mixed with confusion. Instead of a common awakening; protests were moving in all sorts of different directions. And the Vietnam War splintered everything as well.

North and South, young black males were drafted. Those with drug problems and/or a police record stayed on the streets. The guys drafted, who otherwise would have been natural leaders at home, were fucked up by divided loyalties between those to their beleaguered communities and patriotism. So many became either direct casualties or indirect victims to drugs or just to the general craziness of shooting up poor people far away for white generals.

Back to College Interlude

I would never have submitted to the draft. College was a refuge, and I wanted it to put intellectual feet under my radical heart. I didn't succeed.

I recall reading in the library. Next to me was a first-year student I'd heard denounce the pigs at demonstrations. He was reading something called Labor Struggles. I could see revolutionary sugar plums dancing in his eyes. I was reading in Hobbes's Leviathan in the early part where he's describing the uses and abuses of speech:

"To these uses there are also four correspondent abuses. … Fourthly, when they use them to grieve one another, for seeing Nature hath armed living creatures, some with teeth, some with horns, and some with hands, to grieve an enemy, it is but an abuse of speech to grieve him with the tongue, unless it be one whom we are obliged to govern; and then it is not to grieve, but to correct and amend."

I gave a loud chuckle because it seemed to me such an apt way to put it. Labor Struggles looked over to see what I was laughing at and, when he saw Thomas Hobbes, gave me a strange look as if to say, "What the fuck are you doing laughing at that old dry stuff?"

There were vague but potent intuitions somewhere in my head that favorite writers like Thomas Wolfe or Herman Melville must have somehow put into their work the need for radical social transformation. I talked myself and my advisor into a proposal for a paper on Melville combining literary with social science themes. The inexpressible connections I sensed remained inexpressible, and events in any case drained me of energy to try.

In 1968, the Vietnam war was still going full blast, the Democratic Presidential nominating convention was coming to

Chicago, and big anti-war demonstrations were in preparation. I leafleted for the coming demonstrations in South Shore, then a more or less middle-class Jewish community. Nobody would take my leaflets. Finally, an old black woman on the street took one. Then she held out to me a copy of the Jehovah's Witness magazine, The Watchtower. I couldn't refuse it.

A little later on, I was part of a preliminary march through another part of the city. We ended up singing the songs from the play Marat/Sade as we went:

"Marat, we're poor

And the poor stay poor.

Marat, don't make us wait anymore.

We want our rights

And we don't care how.

We want our Revolution, now!"

When the convention finally arrived, thousands of demonstrators gathered for a protest march. The police were out in force and blocked the planned march route. The demonstrators began flowing around the police blockade, and the whole scene broke apart with the police chasing and clubbing knots of demonstrators. The demonstrators in turn broke apart and flowed like water through rapids in the direction of the Convention. I tried to stay near a tv camera, thinking I'd be safer from the police that way. The camera man, himself scared, had no desire for demonstrators near him.

A commission later labeled the whole thing a "police riot." Mayor Daly, famous for his malapropisms, came on tv, his body and voice both shaking with indignation at the commission report: "The police were not there to create disorder. They were there to preserve it."

Later in the school year, demonstrations on campus climaxed with a student occupation of the university administration building. The university quickly announced that demonstrators who continued the occupation would face expulsion. I was there in the administration building when the announcement was made. Listening to the chaotic and, I thought, thoroughly confused arguments, I decided I didn't know why I was there and left. Many people I knew stayed. Instead of completing the coursework I needed for graduation, I watched the disciplinary hearings in dismayed fascination as so many had their studies at Chicago brought to a sudden end, something few of them had really expected. The men were then left in the same dilemma I shortly faced: exposure to the Vietnam draft.

I never finished my course work and never graduated. I ran out of money and, for a short while, half-way managed by delivering telephone directories – you got paid every day. Finally, I called my mother, told her my troubles, and went back to Washington, D.C., to stay with her for a little while. An induction order caught up with me there.

San Francisco and North Beach

It never occurred to me to accept induction. Sarah and John had moved to San Francisco, and I wanted to visit them before refusing. Sarah and John were killing time, working at the Rainbow Health Plan processing claims, uncertain where life was taking them. The offices were on Stockton Street, right near Washington Square Park, about two blocks north of Chinatown, right in North Beach. Sarah and John told me the Plan was hiring, and I got a job there. Before too long, they had moved on. And the job was right around the corner from the bars on upper Grant Avenue.

I had imagined a dramatic confrontation quickly coming to a head between lonely me and the Vietnam draft, ending with my heroic refusal and a jail sentence. Boy, was I off the mark. It took time for the induction order to be transferred to San Francisco and then more time for the physical to be scheduled and rescheduled.

The draft physical, when it finally came about, was an awful experience. I was in my mid-twenties by then, and most of the others were just kids a little out of high school. Regardless of age we were almost all nervous and intimidated as we were herded around in our shorts.

I thought of the story of another guy from the University of Chicago who was proud of how he'd escaped induction. Like me, he had been much older than the others there for the physical. He had waited until toward the end, then cut both his wrists and hurled the blood spurting from them at the other inductees while yelling, "Kill up them lousy Viet Cong." He'd gotten a mental disqualification. Another guy I'd known in the early days of the draft had played gay and been refused. That didn't work for long though. Pretty soon, the army was saying, "So what?"

The officials at the various examining stations all thought every one of us was trying to put some kind of game over on them. They were pretty much right. There was a street freak from Berkeley, skinny, an abscess the size of a dime on one finger and spatters of blood on his shorts. He tried to bum drugs from the bored staff testing us at each station. He was ignored and just passed along with the rest of us from station to station. For all I know, he became one of our boys in uniform. One guy I at first admired because he seemed so much more composed than the rest of us. Toward the end, he revealed he was so calm because he was a literal space case, talking about the situation on Alpha Centauri.

After the exam was complete, everybody was directed to the "Ceremony Room" for induction. By then, they had a regular routine for refusers. After they'd processed the main group, they brought the four or five of us in, read us the induction order, and we refused. One guy said this was the third time for him: after he refused, he'd just get another induction order. There were a couple FBI agents on hand who warned us about the serious crime we were committing, took some personal information, and then let us loose.

There were volunteer lawyers defending draft refusers, and I got one of them. The legal procedures crawled with long intervals between appearance dates. Eventually, I appeared in court before Federal District Judge Lloyd Burke, God bless his memory. I pled no contest, waived a jury trial, and presented a statement expressing not my objection to war in any form (required for Conscientious Objector status) but to the Vietnam War in particular. Judge Burke; who, to my great good fortune, had a liberal attitude, sentenced me to probation on condition I find work equivalent to alternative service for a Conscientious Objector. I said to my lawyer, "Well, I'm working for the Rainbow Health Plan in their Medi-Cal pilot project. Rainbow is a nonprofit, and Medi-Cal benefits the poor." We proposed it, and after a short hesitation, Judge Burke approved it. My heroic witness ended with an enormous piece of luck. So many who thought they had no real choice but to go got screwed up in the head or worse by going.

I had started with what seemed a clear path to perfecting the world I lived in. In the end, it reminded me of a vacation I took in Rio de Janeiro in the 90's. I had a tourist map and wanted to get from one museum to another. I saw it wasn't that many blocks and the route seemed clear on the map. I started walking but somehow took a wrong turn off the main route. I wasn't too worried. The streets I was now on didn't show on the map, but it couldn't be too far to get back. All I had to do was experiment a little to find my way. But instead of getting back on the main route to the museum, I got to a big traffic circle with a big tunnel leading off into a hillside. I tried again and came back to that same traffic circle three times. The last time, a big flatbed truck with troops in the back pulled up, stopped, and the troops jumped off and started deploying. "I'm in the wrong place," I said to myself. I managed to flag a cab. I didn't speak Portuguese, but I showed the driver a slip from my hotel with the hotel's name and address on it. The driver nodded. He gestured out the window where the troops had deployed. He took a pen and drew a skull and crossbones on the back of his hand. Then he took me to my hotel. Judge Burke had been my cab. My job was like the hotel. But who wants to travel just to hide in a hotel? Thank God I could go around the corner to North Beach and its bars.

CHAPTER 6 TONI

Before Toni suddenly jumped into the center of my life, I knew her slightly as part of the North Beach background. Candi, my earlier sweetheart, had seen her panache in the bars and liked it. One summer at a birthday party over in the East Bay, I had seen Toni lolling outside in a bikini. Mildly drunk, I had come over to her, and we had rattled back and forth some. But it was all only the sort of vaguely connected familiarity of one North Beacher with another. Once we had become close, she told me now and then and here and there bits and pieces from her life, and that's really all I can give you here.

But from the stories she told me, I can tell you this: Toni's whole life was a nonnegotiable demand put forward with a combination of charm and desperation. "See, this is the real me. Now deal with it."

Most of us, starting from a baby, put aside parts of ourselves that are too troublesome. The world won't put up with those things, and we are helpless to change things. Gradually, the masks we wear for the world become second nature, and the original one retreats and withers. We flatter ourselves by calling this maturity. It's practical but a sacrifice of vitality.

Toni told me early on that she had started running away from home at three. "When I was little, we had milk trucks, bread trucks, and fresh produce trucks coming to our house. I would hide inside a truck when no one was looking. After a few blocks, I'd show myself. 'Little girl,' the driver would say, 'do you know your telephone number?' 'Yes, but I won't tell you unless you buy me some ice cream.' "

She wouldn't put up with life if it denied her adventure and ice cream. The trouble it took her made her really moody then, and it stayed that way as she navigated life.

She told me she'd had a kid at eleven. "They told me not to kiss, but they never told me not to fuck." Her parents had put her in a home for unwed mothers until she delivered. She said, "It just popped right out. No problems." She had found it a sensual event. The infant had been immediately taken away for adoption. Toni felt deprived of a basic human experience. A basic human experience, to be sure, but at eleven? But it was never in Toni to wait for anything. She was the do/don't girl from beginning to end -- always struggling to catch up with herself while at the same time already in the middle of something new.

In religion, Toni was a kind of free-form mystic. No doctrines except insofar as they grabbed her artist's eye as if they were snippets from one of her boxes of collage material. Her beliefs were like cloud shapes teasing definition.

One time in the Saloon, somebody I knew a little who had worked at Rainbow Health Plan happened by and came in when he saw me there having a drink. He looked around the bar at the bartender and the regulars in there getting wasted. I was pumped because I'd just finished a poem about Toni and had a copy in my pocket. I showed it to him. He read it, but I couldn't read his expression. But I didn't think it was positive. He looked around the bar again. "I don't know," he said, "it just seems to me like a lot of these people in North Beach are just leading wasted lives." "Waste is very ecological," I told him. "Without waste, you can't have wild flowers like Toni."

Chapter 7 North Beach

Huckleberry Finn is an excellent novel. Huck and Jim are fine characters. The Duke and the Dauphin are fine rascals. But the book is nothing without the river. Of course, North Beach is not a river. But still … The bars of North Beach had an inner music that seemed to me a cousin to the slave songs that so moved Frederick Douglass, and I had nothing better to do than learn the words.

North Beach is just north of Chinatown and continues toward Fisherman's Wharf. It's full of bars, restaurants, and alleys with apartment houses in them. It's the old Italian section of San Francisco. Right around Broadway and Columbus, there are many cheap residence hotels. In the 60s, beatniks started populating the neighborhood, including its bars and cheap hotels. When topless nightclubs came along, they made their home along Broadway. If you walked the sidewalk there in the evening, you could hear barkers chanting, "Naked … naked … naked … totally naked."

The Coffee Gallery was a beer and wine bar on upper Grant Avenue, just a couple blocks from my job at the Rainbow Heath Plan. It had a sign above the big front window with a chess piece on it and, now and then, a couple people at the big table inside that window playing chess. I was a casual chess player. I liked dive bars. And that became my first stop in North Beach.

The first time I dropped into the Coffee Gallery for a beer, I saw old Wes putting on one of his rants. I came to learn that these rants were as much a part of him as his skin. This time, he was trying to get a rise out of an old stranger who had happened into the bar to kill time before meeting his daughter at a restaurant. Wes was having no luck getting a rise. The guy was too good-natured.

He scarcely paid any attention to Wes and finally just looked at his watch, swallowed the last of his beer, and left. Wes grumbled to himself about what a doorpost the guy had been.

Wes practiced his tirades, and it was unusual for him to strike out. One time, I went back to the john to take a leak and found Wes drunk, propped against the wall with one arm and leering at himself in the dented metal men's room mirror. "Sonny boy," he said into his bent and twisted image, "Your stupidity amuses me."

When he wasn't insulting somebody, Wes was a good story teller.

He said he was the only person he knew who'd ever been thrown into a bar. He'd gotten into a skirmish in the Coffee Gallery with the wrong person and gotten pushed through the open front window into the street. He'd landed on a passing tourist. The tourist was pissed off and pushed him back through the window.

Wes had a story about being on the bum in New York years ago. He'd been panhandling with another guy, and somebody had given him a dollar. He started to stick it in what he called his "cozy pocket" – the little pocket on a man's trousers on the right side just above the change pocket. As he did so, he discovered a $100. bill there. He'd stashed it as the remainder from blowing off a lot of money on a big drunk, then forgotten about it. "Look what the man just gave me," Wes said, showing off the $100 to his buddy. "Let's go get drunk."

"Not me," said his partner. "If you can get $100, so can I. I'm sticking right here."

Wes also claimed that the parking meters in Nome, Alaska, were on swivels to muffle collisions when cars slid into them on icy days. He claims he'd staggered out of a bar, grabbed a parking meter for support, but instead of supporting him, it just went with him down to the sidewalk. Then it slapped him in the face when he let go of it as he got up.

The first chess game I ever played at that table was with Big Dan – skinny, about 6 foot seven, with weak eyes who would bend way over the chess board, his nose almost touching the pieces. I'd win perhaps one game out of five with him. We were near in age. He'd once had some sort of computer-related job, but the regular job market seemed well behind him. He'd lived for a while at a hippie ranch in the North Bay but was not really a communal type. Dan kept very much to himself. In those early days when I was getting to know him, he was waiting for eligibility for a government check and couldn't afford anything but coffee to drink. After he started getting checks, he was able to get glasses. He must have been an ascetic in a prior life. He almost never asked to borrow and didn't seem to mind living poor. He had a loud yuk-yukking laugh that seemed partly amused, partly nervous. It seemed an embarrassed satire of a laugh, as though apologizing for his amusement.

Then, there was old Larry. Everybody called him old Larry, though not to his face. I think his weak health made him seem a good bit older than he was, and his boozing had aged him more than just the years. I'd guess he was around 50. Dan didn't play bridge until Larry and I taught him the game, but Dan was a natural for games and, not long after taking it up, had surpassed both Larry and me.

Larry topped both Dan and me in life experiences. He had once held down some sort of responsible computer-related job, but long ago. He now got a monthly check. It was enough to buy a few glasses of port at the Coffee Gallery, and now and again, somebody else would buy him one. If someone asked what he wanted to drink, his answer was "a pitcher of port." One time, somebody actually got him one. That pitcher was sort of like the puff of smoke in a magic trick. Larry nearly disappeared under the table.

When I first met him, Larry lived in the Bell Hotel, a cheap hotel on Kearny right across from Clown Alley hamburgers. Most of the tenants got welfare checks, and first of the month theft from the mail boxes was a constant problem. On occasion, I'd crash there on a weekend night when I was too far gone to take the bus. The room was covered with litter, and the bed springs truly had your back. The Bell burned down, and Larry moved on to the New Riviera Hotel right across from Washington Square Park. A great location but a terrible hotel. Larry eventually had a hip replacement. He told me that a long ago operation on one hip had altered his gait, and over time, that had ruined the other one. With his constant boozing, he was a terrible candidate for the replacement surgery. The surgery is pointless unless you rehab diligently, and it ought to have been apparent that he wouldn't. Instead, he wound up bed-confined in his hotel room. The window gave on an air well. People used his room as a corridor, climbing in through the window and out his room door, stealing anything that looked worth it as they came through. He finally was admitted to a county extended care home, never really able to walk again after his surgery.

The bridge game drew a miscellaneous bunch of occasional players. There was Big Gil, one of the bartenders, and his old lady Mary, a blues singer.

Gil was a fine bartender, about 6 foot 4 inches and heavy. Fortunately, he also had a mild temper. When Gil told a drunk it was time to leave, the drunk would take a look at Gil (who was always very calm about it) and decide, yes, it was time to leave.

Gil told a story about a tourist who had come in and had three or four beers without leaving a tip. The tourist ordered one more, and when Gil served it, the tourist asked, "Say, doesn't the bar ever buy a drink here?" Gil answered with a straight face, "I really wouldn't know, sir. I've only worked here for four years." Another time, Gil told me there had been a guy in the bar nursing a beer all through his shift. It was apparent to Gil that the owner had hired the guy to watch to see whether all the money was going into the cash register. Toward the end of his shift, Gil drew draft beers, one for each of them. As he handed the guy his beer he said, "Have one on the house. We're both working for the same man."

When I first started drinking in the Coffee Gallcry, Karl owned it. Not an endearing man, but he did know how to run a Bohemian bar. He sold it and moved to Spain not too long after I became a regular. The place went through a couple other owners in fairly quick succession before Bill bought it. Bill had had a blues bar in the Haight previously and bought the Coffee Gallery primarily as a place to continue putting on the blues. Bill had a partner, but one who rarely showed her face in the bar. I recall one Friday afternoon after work, I was there, and Bill was talking with Lena, a real blues trooper who had had gigs at Bill's bar in the Haight. Now she wanted to sing at the Coffee Gallery.

Lena once told me about singing in a Chicago bar with a roof so bad that the snow was drifting through it.

Bill said, "If it were just me, I'd put you on the calendar in a minute. But I've got a partner. You know how badly you two get along. I can't book you without her approval."

"Maybe if I just talk to her," Lena said.

I wasn't there to see the aftermath, but the story I heard the next day was that Bill's partner had later turned up in the bar. Lena, who had been drinking, decided to talk to her to smooth things over and get a gig. It didn't work out. Instead, Lena, who was a full-bodied woman, wound up punching the partner out. Still in the end, it was ok. Nappy down at the Saloon bought out Bill's first partner, and Lena got her gig.

If you're wondering where all this hanging out was getting me, I didn't want to get anywhere.

The Saloon

The next step into North Beach was the Saloon – full name, the 1232 Fresno Hotel Saloon. When I first started hanging out in North Beach, I'd look in and see some old men sitting on big old sofas in the back beyond the bar. As I later learned, it was Teddy's bar then, an old Italian former boxer. At some point, he sold it to Steve Wertz – or "Nappy" as he was soon nicknamed. Nappy was very short and had the sort of aggressive big ego that short men sometimes have; hence, "Nappy," short for Napoleon. Everybody called him that, though usually not to his face. After Nappy took over, everybody started calling it just "the Saloon."

Nappy instituted a happy hour from 8 pm to 9 pm every night. Draft beer fifty cents, pitchers a dollar, well booze sixty cents. The place was packed nightly. It got so I could look around the packed bar and know almost every face.

During the day, Papa Adolfo tended bar, an old Italian who'd been behind a bar longer than I'd been alive. He loved to have things stirred up on his shifts. He and Wes were shouting buddies, yelling at each other about everything and nothing. I recall one time Wes told Adolfo, "Why don't you go away. Go down the end of the bar. Talk to Lucky Bob." Adolfo barely turned his head to look at Lucky. "Lucky don't talk," he said and continued his digs at Wes.

Papa Adolfo had only one basic rule. He didn't want anyone leaving sober or with any money. If you came in broke, Papa would find somebody to buy you a drink. For good looking women that was easy. They were always welcome. If you were a regular but broke that day, sure, he'd find somebody to pay for you. If you were somebody he knew was broke all the time, best not come in.

Randy, a bartender from Vesuvio, told me a story about how he'd been in the Saloon on one of Adolfo's shifts. Randy, who was at the far end of the bar, saw a trouble-maker he'd often thrown out of Vesuvio come in and take a stool near the door. Randy got Papa Adolfo's attention and told him quietly, "That guy by the window is a trouble-maker. Want me to throw him out for you?" Papa said, "It's ok. I take care of it." There were about four people in the bar between Randy and the trouble-maker. Papa went down the bar stopping at each person saying, "Hey. You doing good today? I want you to have a free drink." He got to the trouble-maker, grabbed the guy's drink off the bar, poured it down the sink, and said, "You get out of here now." It was a shock: the trouble-maker had expected he'd get a free drink too. Instead, he found the whole bar staring at him. He left as ordered. "I would have had to fight him," Randy said.

Adolfo had no scruples when it came to tourists. I heard one time he had a drunk tourist in the bar who wanted to cash a $50.00 Traveler's Check. Adolfo said, "How do I know it's good? I don't think I cash it." The tourist tried showing him lots of ID. Adolfo wasn't persuaded. The tourist said, "I'll buy the whole bar a drink if you cash it for me."

"I don't know. You sign it and let me see."

The tourist signed the Traveler's Check. Papa looked at it doubtfully. "This don't look so good. You better sign another one."

The tourist signed another one. Papa looked at the second one, then back at the first one, back and forth. Finally, he threw both in the register. "I guess one of them is good." The tourist was too drunk to realize what had just happened to him.

After Nappy was a partner at the Coffee Gallery and seeing the blues doing well there, Nappy put music in at the Saloon also, booking many of the same musicians. Nappy reveled in the prestige of owning a money-making bar. He even put up with people playing "Short People" on the juke. He even put up with the time when his bartender, while Nappy was hitting on a pretty tourist, took Nappy's derby off the hook, then, making fun of Nappy's size, knee-walked from behind the bar, out by Nappy and the pretty tourist, tipping Nappy's derby at them, and out the door to have a drink down the street. Life was all going great for Nappy until he got a new girl friend and started doing a lot of coke. In the end he put his business up his nose. The Saloon was closed for several months until Damian, one of the sons of the Chinese family who owned the building, opened up the bar again. Damian, as it happened, was a musician with the San Francisco Symphony. He seemed an improbable bar owner and blues promoter, but it all worked out well. He continued the music, booking many of the same blues players and adding others as time went on. He even eventually put in a recording studio in the basement of the Saloon where some of the groups recorded CDs.

Morning Coffee

My first North Beach friends I made at the table in the front window of the Coffee Gallery playing chess and bridge. Happy hours at the Saloon and Papa Adolfo's shifts there brought me further into neighborhood life. But in lots of ways, it was when I started having my morning coffee in Vesuvio that I really settled in. At night, the neighborhood was putting on a face. In the morning, it was just its natural self.

My friend Mel was a Vesuvio morning regular who always sat at the end of the bar near the window, reading his newspaper and keeping to himself. I got into the habit of sitting on the next stool and likewise reading the morning paper. He liked me, it turned out because I didn't say much to him. He was a good bit deaf and a good bit of a loner besides, and I protected him from people who'd otherwise take that next stool and yammer to him.

He belonged to the seamen's union and told me about one time walking a picket line while chanting "Om mane padme hum," the Buddhist mantra. I think it likely pleased him that nobody else on the line had any idea what it meant. He was a great reader with a wide range. He introduced me to Alexandra David Neel, the French Buddhist practitioner who wrote about her travels in Tibet early in the 20th century. He also read hard-boiled detective novels and Nelson Algren. And a bio of Wittgenstein. He read a book only once and would often pass along the books he was done with to me. It was great, except that Mel was a critical reader and had a habit of tearing out the pages he didn't like.

At sea, he said most sailors liked to put in overtime, but he'd rather read. Shipping out suited his inward-turning nature down to the ground. He told of one bunk mate he had who talked to his sea chest. Mel said to him, "Would you cut out talking to your sea chest?"

"Why? It's mine," the other replied.

It was the kind of argument Mel could appreciate, so he let it be.

Mel told me stories about being a union steward. I asked him, "Being the loner you are, how did you ever get to be the union steward?"

"I was the only one who knew the contract," he said.

If Mel woke up before the bar opened, he would have coffee at a donut shop down the street that opened early. One morning, he was heading from the donut shop to the bar when a young Latino with a knife wanted to rob him. "You'll have to speak up. I'm deaf," Mel said. The kid was confused and decided robbing somebody else would be simpler.

In the Crow's Nest

One time, I was up in the window of the Crow's Nest, smoking weed with the Alice and Lucky Bob. Lucky Bob was called that because he drank Lucky Lager, not because of good fortune. He had come to North Beach about the same time as I did. He was clean-cut then, and not just his hair. He seemed to be just a little younger than me. He joined the bridge game at the front table at the Coffee Gallery -- intelligent, competent, and neither particularly quiet nor talkative. He got a job as a bartender at the Coffee Gallery, then picked up some miscellaneous shifts at the Saloon. Gradually, he withdrew into himself. He pretty much stopped playing bridge and grew a good-sized beer belly. He now talked mostly when he'd been smoking some weed. Like now.

Lucky Bob was looking down at the Saloon and saw Raylette Charles going in. Raylette was a transsexual who'd shown up in the bars about three years ago. She was about six foot tall, slender, with great big strong hands, and a deep, thrilling, lilting voice. Even when she didn't talk loud, you could hear her all over the room. Bob started telling a story about her confrontation with a tourist who was confused and angered by her sexuality. "The tourist was a real pain in the ass. You know they say Raylette carries a razor blade in her wig, and I believe it. She first ignored him, but she finally faced the asshole and said, 'My name is Raylette D. Charles. I am a war veteran. I was a man, and I am a woman. And if you don't shut your filthy mouth, I am ready to cut.' The tourist shut up."

Lucky Bob paused for a toke. "I asked Raylette later, 'What does the D. stand for?' She batted her eyes at me and said, 'Doo-wop, of course, darling.' "

Small, who was shy and in many ways conventional, said, "I don't know about changing your sex like that from what God made you. Is it right?"

Every now and then, Tall, when she was stoned, would reel off a crazy riff, and she did one now: "Honey, you can call me a metrosexual because I've had a whole city in my pussy: long ones and short ones, fat ones and skinny ones, weird ones and straight ones, jive-ass and classical, missionary ones and kinky ones, fast food and banquets, black and white and technicolor. Or if I am a country girl, it's because I've almost had the whole country in there. It's all good, honey. Don't worry about it." She giggled and tousled Small's hair. In lots of ways, Tall treated Small like a little sister. Small didn't really like being dismissed this way, but she didn't say anything more.

Candi

The 4th of July, 1976 came on a Sunday. I didn't have any particular plans, just generally expected a good time. I thought Firebird would be sure to have something doing at Vesuvio. I showed up right at 6 AM, ready for anything. Nothing happened. I got drunk. The more nothing happened, the more drunk I got. Finally, in a foul mood (or as foul as I could manage, drunk as I was), I went home to sleep it off. I came to in the evening and went out again, determined to make up for the bad start to the day. Still, nothing happened except that I got spitefully drunk again. And back to sleep it off again.

Inasmuch as the 4th had been on a Sunday, the 5th was a holiday. I got up and went to Vesuvio again. More nothing. I restrained my boozing enough to put my disgust into verse:

Bicentennial Poem to Commemorate a Rotten 4th of July Followed by a Rotten 5th

With a roll of drums, I marched up my own asshole
To the amazement of cheering thousands.

I wrote it out on a cocktail napkin and was so proud of it I got some notebook paper from Tall and copied it down twice: one copy to keep, the other to show off.

I headed for the Saloon and Papa Adolfo. As I went in, I saw a guy and an attractive girl sharing a joint in the alley. I had started on a Rainier Ale when they came back into the bar and took stools near me. I showed them my patriotic poem. They laughed. andandThen, we started talking. The guy turned out to be a sailor having a good time and wanting to spend more money, but he needed to cash a check. Papa Adolfo was in a dilemma. He had a live one, but he didn't know him and didn't trust a check from him. Seeing how the three of us were getting along, he said, "I tell you what. I cash a check for Bob. You write Bob a check. If he take your check everything ok." The sailor wanted to cash a $50. check. I looked at him. I saw a young sailor in a good mood wanting to spend money on this holiday. My mood had lifted. I went ahead with the proposition. The sailor bought drinks for the girl and me. When those were gone, I bought a round. We drank, talked, and laughed. I had had a bit of a head start on them at Vesuvio, so I couldn't keep up the pace for long, and after 2 or 3 more, I headed back for my apartment to sleep it off. But in a much better mood than yesterday.

That July 5 turned out to be just a seed. Next Friday evening, I saw the girl by herself in the Saloon and started talking to her. Her name was Candi. She was from a small town in northeastern Colorado where she'd married a high school sweetheart. He'd gone into the military, and that had taken them to California. She had discovered that she wasn't really a small-town girl after all, and that didn't fit whatsoever with her husband's view of life, which was strictly bounded by Reveille and Taps. Friction led to divorce which led to explorations, which led to North Beach. Everything was discovery and confusion, and she couldn't get enough of it. She had a good figure and straight brown hair coming down to her shoulder blades. She had a nervous habit of tossing her head and swinging her hair around her shoulders. It wasn't at all unattractive. I bought her some drinks and suggested we go up the street to the Coffee Gallery to listen to some blues. We were there until closing time.

"Last call, ladies and gentlemen, last call for alcohol. If you don't get it now, you don't get it at all."

Then, a few minutes later, the lights went up, and, "Drink 'em up. It's closing time. Hotel, motel – I don't care what you do, but you can't do it here. Drink 'em up, drink 'em up, and out the door. That's it, that's all, ladies and gentlemen."

It turned out Candi had no place to stay that night. I offered to bring her back to my place. She looked at me, looked down for a moment, swung her hair, and said ok.

I had just time to get a pint of whisky at the Korean grocery on the corner, then to my apartment. We drank and talked some more. She was still shedding the small town, she told me. She'd been in Civic Center plaza and had seen a wino passed out on a bench. She shook his shoulder, and he only muttered and turned away. She called 911 for an ambulance. She was indignant over how blasé the people in the plaza were. Then the paramedics arrived, rousted the wino, and berated her for wasting their time. The wino muttered, "Stupid damn bitch," at her as he shambled away.

But then there was North Beach. She'd passed by the Saloon peeked in the bar. Papa Adolfo had called to her, "Come in, come in. See these gentlemen here? They all want to buy you a cocktail." She'd come in, pretty soon had picked the sailor as her favorite, and then I came along and solved the check cashing problem. It's a wonderful world.

At my apartment that Friday night, we said, "Blah, blah, blah…" as we leaned against each other on my sofa. I had my arm around her. We kissed a bit. A pause came. She swung her hair (although we were really too close for her to swing it well). "Do you think we're inhibited," she asked. The question removed mine and hers as well. Much as we'd both been drinking, we didn't accomplish much that night but did better in the morning.

Candi's life then had no order at all, but she was too busy with it to care. She'd been cadging places to stay from various people – a few she'd known before, more that she was meeting now. She said she was looking for a job, but that was mostly just something she said when somebody asked her what she did. After a week or so, she moved in with me. All her stuff at that time amounted to 2 suitcases and 3 or 4 moving boxes. During the week, I went to work, and she went exploring – walking across the Golden Gate Bridge to Sausalito, checking out Golden Gate Park, Baker Beach, Lands' End, stuff like that. Or exploring the bars of North Beach, a project that I'd already spent 6 years doing and still was working on. Weekends we'd do something or other together. More bars, maybe out in the open during the day, maybe walking around at night. She loved the Redwood park outside the Transamerica Pyramid, hugging the trees there, maybe up to Coit Tower, looking out toward the Bay Bridge, maybe down to the Ferry building, maybe into Chinatown, and checking out the little alleys.

Candi and I got along well but never seemed to settle into a common life. She was certainly open to experience but at the same time always had a reserve about her. She had a way of falling into a kind of dreamy, absorbed, abstracted look, as if something about you or something you'd said had touched something deep within her, or as if she was wrapped in a beautiful fantasy, or as if she was wondering what she wanted to eat for supper tomorrow. I learned it might be any of these. The guy she was with – me included, even when I really knew better – almost always assumed one of the first two. It was part of her charm.

Candi's beauty was in her spirit of adventure – people, places, trips, emotions – all shuffled together like a deck full of jokers. She pulled it off because nobody wanted to take her adventures away from her. She charmed the mix she moved through into giving her a break. She somehow managed to have all kinds of good times and keep a little common sense in her back pocket. She told me one time that soon after she was divorced, when shewent to a party, she would immediately ask, "Where's the drugs?" You can get away with that kind of life if you hold a joker.

After she'd been living with me two or three months, she really did start looking for a job. The post office in the late 60s and early 70s had been a haven for people who wanted a job but hadn't much interest in working. She lucked into such a haven, an inside job at a local branch, getting it just before that kind of opportunity closed. She had a great interest in San Francisco history, and I had made her a gift of a book of Arnold Genthe's photos of 19th-century Chinatown. "I really love it," she said, "but I just don't have time to look at it except when I'm at work."

Once she was getting her own check she found herself her own place. It wasn't that we didn't like each other anymore, but it was a big world, and she wanted her own independent life in it. Besides, she'd taken to Alex, an admirer of Langston Hughes and a poet who wrote about black consciousness. He fascinated Candi with his combination of sensitivity, wit, and militance. He had frizzy hair that he wore in a bush and a kind of light dusty brown complexion. After they had taken up with one another, Alex got one of those DNA analyses to learn more about his ancestry. He had hopes for African princes. Instead, it turned out his DNA was a sort of garden-variety Mediterranean mix. It shook his life. He wrote a new poem, "Black Like Me – O, Never Mind." His sulking took the mystery out of the relationship for Candi. She continued her explorations in other directions. Before too long she'd taken up with a Mexican playing minor league baseball in Fresno. He spent the off-season in San Francisco. Candi and I remained good friends, drinking together, taking walks, and going on outings now and again, but she was very chaste once the romantic fire no longer burned with someone.

Dolly and Tibet

A new bar, Gullivers, opened up across the street from the Saloon. When I first arrived in North Beach, the place had been the MDR (for Minimum Daily Requirement) and had served sandwiches and had beer on tap. I recall they had a split pea soup you could eat with a fork. The MDR had disappeared, and a couple of bars had replaced it before Gullivers came along. Gullivers ran an early morning shift, and Firebird moved over from Vesuvio to take it. Dolly pretty soon teamed up with Firebird to offer a cheap breakfast on the weekends. Fried eggs or simple sandwiches out of a small electric skillet. It couldn't compete with a regular restaurant's breakfast, but it was cheap, and you didn't have to leave the bar.

Dolly, of course, sounds like a woman's name, but in fact, Dolly was a guy. Dolly was a corruption of "Dalai." He maintained he was the Dalai Lama of Tibet.

Dolly had originally come to Silicon Valley, where he got a job as a draftsman at Hewlett Packard, making detailed drawings of computer circuit boards and the like. He met a young nurse, married her, and started a family. But he discovered that wasn't the life for him. He started taking odd shifts as a fill-in bartender, then, seeing a need, started a side business selling bar supplies – juices, cocktail napkins, glasses, peanuts, beef jerky, stuff like that. That took him to North Beach, and he ended up giving up his job with Hewlett Packard and moving to San Francisco. His wife wasn't happy about it, but nurses were much in demand, and it was easy for her to find a San Francisco job.

I don't know when he decided he was the Dalai Lama. All the time I knew him, he took lithium to control his bipolar tendencies. He wasn't doing LSD during the years I knew him but had before that. "It's the king of dope," he said. Maybe it started with an LSD vision. But by the time I knew him, the idea had morphed into a kind of game. He had named the van he used for his bar supply business "Tibet", Billboard Fred painted a mandala on the side, and he got a Ken doll and had Mary Thomas make him tiny monk's robes for it. He installed it in Tibet where it reigned as the Dolly Lama of Tibet. As for the Dalai Lama in Nepal, Dolly said, "How can he be the real Dalai Lama? He's never even been in "Tibet." I know the geographical Tibet has high mountain passes, and I read that native travelers would shout, "The Gods have won!" when they reached the top of one pass and before descending into the next valley. But I truly wonder whether they got as high as the highs I got with Dolly in the back of "Tibet."

Dolly and his wife had a place out in the avenues. His marriage was a troubled one. "It was great at first, but the more I got to be myself, the worse we got along," he said. "I mean, we do care for each other, but we don't get along much anymore. And the less I'm home, the better it is. She complains about me not being home for days at a time, but it's worse if I am. She's just not being logical about it." Dolly had an air mattress in the back of Tibet, and sometimes, he spent the night there. After he started sharing Firebird's morning shift at Gullivers, however, he started sharing Firebird's place quite often. Dolly was a good bit of a tomcat, but in the end seemed largely to settle down splitting time between his wife and Firebird. It became a kind of double domesticity. But it wasn't a perfect arrangement. One Thanksgiving, Gullivers threw a Thanksgiving feed. Somebody asked Firebird, "Where's Dolly?" Firebird gave a "What do you mean asking me that?" kind of stare before flatly answering, "He's home with his wife and family."

Dolly got to feeling lousy and even missing some shifts. It took him some time before he finally went to the doctor. His fears came true. He had an inoperable cancer, and it was moving fast. He only lasted a couple months after that doctor visit and spent almost all of that in a sort of home jail with his wife and daughters. His wife, a religious woman, arranged a conventional religious funeral for him. As it happened, I'd been out to his home in the avenues a few times to watch football games on tv. I got invited to the memorial as a sort of lone concession to North Beach. It was awful. The minister delivering the eulogy kept looking down at a notecard to remind himself of Dolly's name (Gerald Hapsworth). Dolly's younger daughter, about 12, fidgeted all through the service and made little faces when the minister looked at his notecard. For me, that was the only human part of the whole thing. But it satisfied his wife. All respectable. Nothing about Tibet.

Firebird arranged a separate memorial for him on Mount Tam. Before Dolly died, she had gotten into Tibet and rescued Ken, the Dolly Lama, and we buried it on Mt. Tam. Everybody had a joint: you couldn't pass it. Firebird cried. Others giggled as they toked and told stories about Dolly. At one time he had been a relief bartender at the Grant and Green. There was a phone booth right outside. One weekend morning (this was before Gullivers), Dolly had gotten into the Grant and Green with his keys, then opened up a bar in the phone booth outside. There was a little shelf right below the phone, and on it Dolly put a half-empty/half-full bottle of whiskey, a rocks glass, and a bar rag. He stood right beside the phone booth, wearing a bow tie. The event was completed when Terrible Tommy, a seaman who'd just gotten off a ship, drank up the rest of the bottle of whiskey and passed out. He became the first and only 86 from that bar, or would have been if it had been possible to move him. He was big and pure dead weight. That was far from being the only story.

Dolly's death put Firebird into a tailspin for some time. She told me about it later. "It was really bad. I just didn't feel like doing nothing. Finally, I decided I needed to see a shrink, but I couldn't afford it. Caroline heard me complaining and told me I could borrow her Medi-Cal card. She even made me an appointment. You know how crazy Caroline is. I should have known better than trust her to do anything right, but I had to do something.

"So the appointment's at 450 Sutter. More doctors there than birds in the trees. The doc Caroline set me up with is in a little office with a tiny waiting room and about 3 or 4 people already in it. I go up to the receptionist. I'm nervous because I'm using Caroline's Medi-Cal card. The receptionist just looks at it and says, 'What's your problem?' I don't know what to say. I don't want to announce my business in front of these strangers in the waiting room. The receptionist doesn't have time for nonsense. 'What's your problem?' she says again.

"I lean over close to her ear and whisper, 'I can't cope.'

" 'What,' she says, giving me a weird look.

" 'I can't cope.' I whisper again.

" '**What?**' she says.

" '**I can't cope,**' I yell.

"Now she looks really weird. 'What's that got to do with your feet?' she says.

"That crazy bitch Caroline sent me to a podiatrist. O, well. Maybe it was for the best. It sort of snapped me out of it. And it makes a hell of a story."

Over the years, Tibet had grown temperamental about how it started, and Dolly had developed a complicated routine he went through. After he died, nobody could get it running again. Finally, Billboard Fred made Dolly's widow a lowball offer for it. She took it, and Fred had Tibet towed to a mechanic to fix it. Afterwards, he added a portrait of Dolly with a monk's hood to the mandala he'd painted years ago on the outside of Tibet and so Dolly and Tibet continued to be a presence in North Beach.

Across the River

Poetry in North Beach had a heyday with the Beatniks. Allen Ginsberg is probably the best-known of those poets, but Bob Kaufman was an excellent one and stayed in the neighborhood until his death in 1986. As it happened, I had read and liked his work before ever coming to San Francisco. Early on, around 1970, when I was playing bridge at the front table in the Coffee Gallery, one of the players pointed at a black man sitting at a table. He was shaking all over, head and hands. His feet were coming out of his busted shoes. "That's Bob Kaufman," my bridge-playing friend said. "O, shit," I said. He looked like nobody would ever want to look.

Kaufman went up and down over the years. At times, he even had a kind of stylishness and swagger to him, but he was never during those years a whole man. For a long while, he scarcely spoke except to bum cigarettes and to recite miscellaneous snatches from T. S. Eliot's "The Love Song of J. Alfred Prufrock." The legend was that he had taken a vow of silence after John Kennedy's assassination. I have always discounted that legend. It sounded too romantic an idea to me.

One drunken Christmas, I happened to be on the next stool to Kaufman at the Coffee Gallery. I turned to him and said, "Bobby, you've really written some beautiful poetry." "Don't remind me," he said.

Gradually, the list of bars that would serve him shrank to just one, and it wasn't Vesuvio. In fact, Kaufman's name was one of six in an 86 list in cement on the sidewalk right outside the door to Vesuvio. Still, Kaufman would frequently come just inside the door during Firebird's shift and bullshit a little with her. She would always ask him, "Bobby, when are you going to finish my poem."

"The Firebird is across the river… "he would declaim.

"I know, Bobby, I know. But when are you going to finish it?"

He would just repeat, "The Firebird is across the river… "and head out the door.

One morning, they went through this, but this time, when Firebird asked when he was going to finish her poem, he recited,

"The Firebird is across the river…

Some things have never been completed,

Because they were never meant to be completed.

The Firebird is across the river…"

All of North Beach was across the river. That was its freedom and why it made such a good home for me.

"Sorrow is better than laughter, for by the sadness of the countenance, the heart is made better." *Ecclesiastes 7:3* I look around at the faces in my North Beach bars. There are many doused in sorrow. It is a kind of bedrock. To be sure, there are false fronts that don't fool anybody. There are trills and frills and ups and downs. There is also in various disguises a kind of stubborn savor for the taste of life that I defy you to express clearly.

CHAPTER 8 TONI GROWS THE LIMBO SHIFT

Toni had run into Bill Quack and the idea that she would take over the Limbo Shift just sort of popped up between them. Then, the idea of recruiting Badges to work the door also came to her pretty much spontaneously. That was how Toni did things. She followed her impulses, then ran to keep up with how they developed.

I have to say the Limbo Shift with Toni behind the bar and Badges at the door turned out to be a great combination. It was an on-and-off, now-and-then kind of thing, a rhythm North Beach knew well. Badges gave Toni security, and how many places feature a dakini with a heavy pour behind the bar? The nights she did it, she usually opened about an hour after closing time – enough time for the bar to empty and to give the regular crew time to relax a little and to clean up a little. It would usually run for a couple or three hours. Musicians frequently showed up – living ones to unbend after a gig and dead ones – and there are a lot of those in North Beach – to hang out and sometimes to play a little. Sometimes, Toni would get out from behind the bar and dance.

To be sure, the Limbo Shift wasn't a realistic project. Bill Quack, living and dead, had never been realistic, but his was just a kind of neighborhood screw-up unrealism. Toni's was more complicated. If a project came to her, she took it where it led and kind of played dodgeball with realism. And when you get down to it, it's not so simple to say what realism is. It's not realistic to stick altogether to the actual. That leaves out everything potential, and who would deny that there are such things as real potentials? Even ones that don't get actualized. And, to speak truth, what gets actualized is almost never pure. There are almost always other possibilities hiding in a closet or behind a curtain, waiting to get into the action somehow. Or they show up in dreams, and dreams, especially the most troublesome ones, have a way of somehow sticking pins into reality, as if into a voodoo doll, and changing it in ways hard to understand.

And it's not just negative. What would <u>Mid-Summer Night's Dream</u> be without Bottom's dream? He describes it after his ass's ears and his affair with Titania, the Faery Queen, have both disappeared into the forest mists:

"I have had a most rare vision. I have had a dream—past the wit of man to say what dream it was. Man is but an ass if he go about to expound this dream. Methought I was—there is no man can tell what. Methought I was, and methought I had—but man is but a patched fool if he will offer to say what methought I had. The eye of man hath not heard, the ear of man hath not seen, man's hand is not able to taste, his tongue to conceive, nor his heart to report what my dream was. I will get Peter Quince to write a ballad of this dream. It shall be called 'Bottom's Dream' because it hath no bottom. "

The Limbo Shift, whether it had a bottom or not, had a dakini behind the bar.

We didn't discuss it, and Toni didn't really decide to do it, but she just more or less automatically moved back in with me on Broadway. We were getting along, it was convenient to the Saloon, and she needed somewhere to put her art stuff and to work on it. It was all perfectly natural.

Toni told me the kind of color show she'd put on when she first appeared to me in Chicago (and then disappeared more or less the same way) had been a first for her. She said it just felt natural, so she did it. Now, she found herself turning colors as she danced during the Limbo Shift. She started concentrating on the flow of mood, energy, and color so she could work with it. "I don't control it. That's not the idea. I just sort of work with it. It doesn't control me, and I don't control it. But ain't it grand." And she brought out a brief sort of bright red whole body flush for just a moment. "See."

She was always wound up after her shifts. It was no wonder. I had a doorman for a roommate for a while, and it always took him a few hours to wind down after a weekend shift. He'd come back to the apartment with the bartender, and the two of them would sit there for a couple hours or more, swapping stories about the night and having a few drinks. "What's with these people? Where is their integrity?" my roommate would exclaim. It was a favorite question of his. And indeed, working the door on the weekend you can find plenty of situations that raise it. Like the guy one night who got so drunk he could barely stand, and, when George told him he had to go, insisted that he owned the bar. George escorted him out and stuck him in a cab. But the cabbie got only a block away before he changed his mind and put the drunk out on the sidewalk again.

Toni had never been behind the bar before and wasn't used to a bunch of people making demands on her at once. She wasn't shy. She liked showing off her dancing, but at the same time, her concentration was inward on the dancing, and she told off anybody who interrupted it. Otherwise, she was at her best one on one. She generated an immediate intimacy with people she talked to and disregarded everybody else. She was ok as long as it was just people she knew in the bar, but otherwise, she might blow up. In either case it took a lot of winding down afterwards. Sometimes,

the energy she carried back from the bar she could put to work
doing her art. But not often. Mostly, she was just aggravated and
had to let it wear off.

One time, she came back and pointed to a painting on the wall.
It was a big acrylic abstract; the paint mostly dripped onto the
canvas. It wasn't framed. The canvas was just stretched over a big
box-like frame, and there was about a 3-inch margin where the
canvas was stretched back around the edge. The margin was
painted, too. The colors were a deep blue, black, red, orange, and
white.

There was a story behind the painting. I had gotten it from
Steve Grant, a guy I used to play bridge with now and then in
North Beach. I had been to his hippie wedding years ago in Muir
Woods, most of the people in Renaissance costumes. He had gone
on to have two very nice children -- little girls. The painting had
hung in Steve's apartment, and he knew I liked it. He'd gotten it
from the artist, Big Will Wallace, a friend of his, and, through
Steve, I had also gotten to know Big Will and his studio space in
Project Artaud. Big Will was a disabled ex-longshoreman turned
hippie artist. Besides the acrylic abstracts, he made ceramic beads
that had the appearance of natural stones, though with unusual
colors. He'd roll different colored clays together in his huge hands,
shape them into beads, fire them, then tumble them for days until
they had the natural smoothness of river rocks. Neither his
paintings nor his beads made him but a little bit of money.
Basically, he lived off a disability check.

Steve eventually moved into Project Artaud himself and got
the role of studio manager, collecting the rents from the different
live-in artists like Big Will. Steve's life had taken a bad turn, and
he'd ended up disappearing with a bunch of the rents he'd

collected. Before that, he'd sold me Big Will's painting. Will told me later about the time he thought he'd seen Steve up the street – Steve had distinctive bushy red hair. Will had come up behind him, put a hand on the guy's shoulder, and spun him around. But wrong guy. Will apologized: "You aren't who I thought you were." The guy, still trembling a little, looked up at Big Will and said, "Thank God."

I'd taken Toni out to visit Will at Project Artaud a time or two. He normally would not explain anything about his paintings but paid us a compliment by telling us, "It's a forest fire during a storm." The white streaks were lightning bolts. Now Toni pointed at it and said, "I'm going to do some speed. I want to feel like that."

There was an incident with Alice Small one night. Billy Bones was there, a blues singer who'd appeared regularly at the Saloon before he OD'd a few years ago. The guitarist and keyboard guy from his old group had come in after a gig to wind down. He saw them there and joined them. After a few drinks, they decided to do one of his regular numbers from the old days "So Fucking What?" The chorus went,

> So fucking what?
> I gotta get out of this rut.
> It's giving me a pain in the butt.
> So fucking what!

Maybe you can guess what the verses were like. Small liked it. Actually, it was a favorite of mine too. Small clapped hard and yelled for them to do it again. While Billy was playing, I noticed Toni breaking out in black spots on her face. They got worse when

Small started clapping and yelling to play it again. I think Billy must have noticed Toni too. In any case, he did the chorus once more, then sat down for another drink. Small still wanted more. Toni called her over and spoke to her. "Don't ask for that anymore on my shift. I don't like it."

"O, c'mon. I never get to hear it anymore. It's my favorite."

"Well, you're not going to hear it anymore on my shift either. I told you. I don't like it."

"This is my neighborhood. I should be able to hear my favorite song."

"I told you, not on my shift. Watch it. I don't want to 86 you."

Toni always hated Billie Holiday's "God Bless the Child." I guess she thought of it as a kind of sloppy reverse sentimentality. It wasn't the sort of thing she wanted to discuss. "I just hate it. That's all." "So Fucking What?" seemed to get the same reaction from her.

Billy didn't mean to provoke her, and I think he noticed Toni's reaction and got the message. Like I said, he just sat down and had a few more drinks, hanging out with his buddies. He and Toni didn't talk about it and there didn't seem to be any need. Small grumbled a little to herself, then left. The whole thing didn't seem to amount to much – a tempest in a pitcher of beer maybe.

On the whole, Small was a quiet person who kept pretty much to herself. She'd giggle and chatter when she was on grass or sometimes get nervy and show a little temper when she was speeding, but everybody was used to seeing her moods now and then. Years ago she'd had an intense relationship with a blues player from Texas. It was before I got to North Beach, but Tall told me about it in snatches as we got to know one another. "He dumped her and went back to Texas. He was just a junkie to hear himself talk," Tall said. "He liked to have an intense relationship because it gave him a chance to talk about himself. Small didn't know any better. She's shy, and she thought because he told her all about himself, it meant there was something deep. The way I heard it, music wasn't working out for him in Texas either, and he ended up getting busted for armed robbery."

Tall said that Small used to play with her (Tall's) kids. Small was about 10 years older than the kids, but they still got along fine. It was a relationship with no pressure on either side. Then, after the kids moved out on their own, the two Alices got the Crow's Nest. The two soon became "The Alice". Small used to do house cleaning off and on, and while I was living on Romolo, I got her to clean it for me now and then. I'd give her an advance on the job; she'd use it to get some speed, then she'd zip right through the job. She wasn't meticulous, but then I'm not either, so it worked out. One time after Toni moved in with me, Toni had left a mask she was making sitting on the sofa. It was a paper mache Cleopatra-like life mask of herself. Small while she was cleaning up accidentally sat on it and flattened it. Toni took it with a good grace, all things considered, and in the end, Toni was able to repair it pretty well. It was lucky Small was small. But it left relations between the two uneasy. There might have been a big blow-up, except that they were both such good friends with Tall.

After Texas left, Small got a dog, a good-sized good-tempered animal she named Adam. Adam seemed to satisfy her needs for a deep relationship. The bars in North Beach are usually pretty loose about dogs in the bar during the day, and Adam became almost as much a regular in the Saloon as Small was. Damian, I think perhaps to appease the local beat cops, had put up a sign in the Saloon in big block letters:

NO DOGS IN THE BAR

NO ILLEGAL DRUGS

NO MOTORCYCLE PARKING IN THE ALLEY

I have a snapshot that Bill Quack took of Small, zonked out, with a big grin on her face, leaning against the wall below that sign with Adam at her feet. The sign said, "No, No, No," and everything about Small said, "Yes, Yes, Yes." That snapshot is a favorite of mine. It doesn't hurt it any that Small, had a good trim figure, and her shyness didn't keep her from carrying it well. She was part Chinese, part Native American, and part Pilipino, and she carried that mix very nicely.

One night, Jerry C., Toni's first husband, a jazz sax player, came in to play a set. I remember when she heard of his death. It had been common news in the neighborhood that he'd been in the hospital, but no details. Then a friend phoned Toni to tell her that he was dead. Heart, I think. It knocked Toni onto the floor in tears. Toni had told me the story more than once of how, after an estrangement, she had passed by a bar and heard Jerry C's sax coming out of it. She'd been overjoyed both at the sound and to know he was right there now. She'd gone straight in, and it ended well. Now, looking at Toni as she watched Jerry C. set up for some reason made me remember – misremember actually – some lines from a G. K. Chesterton story:

> As the red sap is to the summer trees
> Is the red red gold to the Ogilvies.

Anyhow, Jerry started to play, and Toni came out from behind the bar to dance, all red and golden. It was quite a moment. But the mood broke when Jerry's last wife came in. I'd seen her occasionally around the neighborhood before. She seemed a very plain woman with none of Toni's flamboyance. But maybe Jerry C. had finally wanted a rest from that. Anyhow, her entrance broke the mood. Jerry played one more number, all red, hot, and sour, like kimchi. Toni just went back behind the bar and served drinks.

Toni had told me about how she and Jerry C. had gotten together. Toni had been an underage waif making it into the bars on her bravado and ability to latch onto some guy who would swear she was 21. She had heard Jerry C. playing one night and loved it. By closing time, she had ditched the guy she'd latched onto and had no place to stay. Jerry C. had taken pity on her and offered to put her up on his couch. She was delighted. At his apartment, his then old lady had raised a stink about his bringing Toni with him. There was a big quarrel, and in the end, Jerry C. had announced, "I'm sleeping with Toni." It had broken the attachment between him and his old lady, and Toni jumped into the hole it had made in his life.

Toni told a story about how, soon after they were living together, a guy had shouted up at their window, "Is Jerry there?" Thinking him a friend of Jerry's, Toni had replied, "No, not right now. But he should be back soon." Proud of her new domesticity, she had invited him up for coffee. He had one cup, then two. Still no Jerry. Finally, he looked over at Jerry's horn sitting over in a corner, picked it up, said, "Well, it doesn't matter. I'm just here to repossess his horn anyway," and walked out. Toni was devastated and afraid to tell Jerry, but there was no way to avoid it. He blew up, of course, but finally had the good grace to laugh it off.

After the shift, I walked back to Broadway with Toni, who was in a mixed mood. At home she took out a collage in progress and worked at it for a little, but it didn't seem to be going anywhere. She finally put down the photos she'd been trying in different positions and stared at her work disconsolately. "I don't know," she said. "I just don't know if it's worthy." She put it all away and came over and gave me a kiss. Usually, the small hours in San Francisco are cool and full of fog. One hot like this was rare.

The growing popularity of the Limbo Shift had its problems. As long as it was essentially just a North Beach party and only now and then, the cops winked at it. It was still only now and then, but it was nonetheless growing. The musicians gradually became not just a North Beach crowd but also from other parts of the city. That drew band followers also. Badges screened them some, but it was hard. One friend would get a friend of his or hers in, then that friend, another, and so on. One asshole who wrote a music column for one of those throw-away papers got in and wrote about what a cool thing it was. He thought he was disguising what he was writing about, but it was easy to put together. Publicity like that was dangerous. Toni closed the shift down for a couple months to calm things back down. They did calm down, but after she started doing the shift again, the popularity started to build again as before. It was a problem. Then there was the night Small made a big scene.

Small – I just call her Small here for short – the way most people did when she wasn't around – but she didn't like it. Alice Small was alright or Alice. But she thought just "Small" was belittling and she'd tell you so every time someone said just

"Small." But she's not around right now, so – Small got her politics from two sources: Leon and Red.

Small had gotten into the habit of going to poetry readings, and Leon was a regular. He was very short, not quite a midget, but still just a little shorter than Small. Maybe it was a short man's Napoleon complex, but whatever the origin, his poetry was all about the coming Revolution against the capitalist oppressors. He would shout it passionately, gesturing hard with his right fist pumping above his shoulder. His mother had named him Frank, but he took Leon from Leon Trotsky. "I am the permanent Revolution." He would proclaim. He liked Small's dog, Adam, and that was always a plus with Small. And then she seemed to have a taste for intense people who liked to talk about themselves. And Small was acutely sensitive about her Chinese, Native American, Pilipino mix – it wasn't a common one anywhere and I can't think of anyone else like her who hung out in the North Beach bars. Leon assured her over and over that capitalists were the cause of poverty and racism and that after the Revolution, the oppressed races and colors would have their day.

Red was nicknamed for his red hair, not for his politics. In fact, he was a sarcastic libertarian loner who was big on guns. He lived for a long time in the Tower Hotel on upper Grant Avenue, and I heard stories of him getting drunk and shooting his revolver off into the ceiling, neither knowing nor caring if there was anybody upstairs. But he was intelligent and not a bad person otherwise. North Beach people gave each other a lot of slack – and it was needed. He got Small to clean up for him from time to time. He liked Adam, and he liked to recite his gun liberty Bible, and those two things – liking Adam and loud opinions -- went a long way with Small.

If Small felt slighted, her revolutionary politics and belief in guns came to the surface. She was mostly at ease around the people she knew – and that knew her – in North Beach, but around strangers and particularly when she was speeding, she was too likely to have an outbreak of opinions.

Then, one night, Small headed in on Toni's shift just to talk to one of the musicians. She was going to clean his apartment and wanted to get her advance and confirm when to do it. Adam came padding in after her. A busybody asshole in a suit tapped her on the shoulder and pointed to the "**No Dogs…**" sign.

Suits aren't automatically bad. I used to head into the Saloon for a drink after work, still in my suit. (I was notorious for wearing a suit weekdays and looking like a bum on weekends.) Young chicks in jeans and work shirts who'd spent all of 30 minutes in North Beach would look at me and say, "What are _you_ doing in this bar?" pronouncing _you_ to rhyme with eewww that you say when you smell something bad. A moment later, they'd be asking, "Are you a lawyer?" And there were some others, though not many, who wore suits in the Saloon. Still, it was unusual, particularly on the Limbo Shift.

Small went off on a rant: "You capitalist racists can't order me around. Adam is better than you are. You're a capitalist dog. You won't be the boss after the Revolution. The people will be the boss. Guns are the answer to pig dogs like you. Guns are the only answer."

Adam, usually so peaceful, growled at the asshole. It was scary because Adam was a big dog. Badges came up behind Small and put his hands on her shoulders. "You can't talk like that on the Limbo Shift," he said and started to steer her outside. Small resisted only momentarily, then let herself be guided outside. She continued to protest, "Guns are the only answer."

Toni had grabbed the asshole's drink off the bar and poured it in the sink. "Get the hell out," she said to him. She had turned an awful black and purple, her eyes red. The snake's tail rattled, something I'd never seen before. The asshole, already shaken by Adam's growl, was now completely unnerved. He left talking to himself in justification: "Crazy people. No class. Law and order. I won't be the one who's shot. Law and order."

Toni had told me about how one time – I can't remember the circumstances – she had been chased by a cop. She had had a good lead on him, and the cop, puffing, had called out after her, "Halt in the name of the law." Toni said she had found this command so funny that she almost stopped running. I was reminded of that now, but, in the circumstances, it had no power to amuse.

Toni had to end that shift right afterward. Nobody had any spirit to continue anyway. The story was all over North Beach the next day. And who knew who the asshole might talk to or what he might do. Toni had to close down the Limbo Shift again for a time.

Tall was upset when she heard. Tall had come up to my apartment to get something from Toni. She sat down and started telling us about the talk she had had with Small. She seemed to be quoting herself verbatim, which shows how urgent it had been and how it had burned into her mind.

"Honey, you know you're a part of me, but I have to tell you – you can't go off like that on the Limbo Shift. You're all in the wrong place right now. It's like the sign for cars going up the freeway off-ramp: 'TURN BACK. YOU ARE GOING THE WRONG WAY.' You got to. I know you think it's all capitalism and racism, but you got to live in this real world here. People in North Beach here have known you for years and years, and you don't want to lose them. They are what you got in life. You can't do stuff that's going to fuck them over. Acting like that, you're going to get the Limbo Shift shut down. Honey, we know you for you inside out. You got to find a way to live with yourself and the people here who know you."

Tall paused for a moment, then continued, "I think about Small. You know, Texas wasn't really all that bad. I mean, he wasn't a bad blues guitarist. He was just full of himself, and then things started going bad for him. And Leon and Red. They're not terrible people. But Small likes somebody, and she just picks their crazy side."

Toni said, "It can be like that. You just want too hard for things to make sense. Lots of times, things make sense in different ways, but they can't both be right. I don't know. You just have to play it by ear. At least, I do." Toni gave one of her shy little girl embarrassed smiles as she often did with people she trusted. "You go crazy otherwise."

"Small just picks somebody else's craziness and makes it her pet," Tall said.

Good advice is hard to stand. Small had stormed out and didn't come home for a day or so. I've felt much the same in similar situations. Leon, of course, was no help. But outside of Leon and Red, Small was getting no support. On the contrary. In the end she had enough sense to make apologies, grudging though they were. And they were grudgingly accepted, though with lots of warnings about what would happen if she did it again.

Damian was alarmed. He was afraid the Limbo Shift would get his bar closed down. It wasn't an unreasonable fear. Toni told me about the heart-to-heart he'd had with her. She had always made him nervous even before she was a dakini and now even more so. Dragons have a lot of authority with Chinese people, and Toni was close enough to a dragon – especially when she lost her temper – that he was a bit afraid of her.

Her temper was like her sexuality, her color dancing, and her art. She didn't control it, but she did work with it. If she was carried away, it was in a direction she consented to. And she was very conscious of the effect she had on other people.

She explained that the Limbo Shift was to save the people of North Beach and the terrible karma he would incur if he shut it down. She went all out, showing at once her charm, her sexuality (which disturbed Damian), and her temper (which disturbed him even more). She said she would shut the Limbo Shift down for a while until things were cool, but then she had to open it up again. I think he read that as a threat of magical spells. In the end, he gave in. Things were papered over all around.

Chapter 9 Toni and Me at Romolo

The Romolo Apartment

Toni lived with me in my Romolo apartment for something like seven years.

The first place I had lived in San Francisco was a room near Sarah and John not far from the Fillmore district; then out to the Mission for a while. But I was working and hanging out in North Beach, so when Bill, the owner of the Coffee Gallery, and his old lady Ellie needed to replace a roommate, I moved in with them. It was two bedrooms, a living room, kitchen. San Francisco – and North Beach in particular – is full of little alleys with apartment houses in them. Sometimes, even the alleys have alleys. Romolo Alley runs between Broadway and Vallejo and intersects with Fresno Alley, which runs between Grant and Kearny. It's a little pocket right in the heart of North Beach. I liked to tell people I had two ways to give directions to my apartment, depending on the impression I wanted to make. Either, "Go to the Trieste Coffee Shop at Grant and Vallejo (where they sing opera sometimes), then down Fresno Alley to Romolo," or "Go to the dirty bookstore right near Broadway and Columbus and turn north up Romolo Alley." Officially, the dirty bookstore was Broadway Cigars and Liquors, but it was universally known in the neighborhood as the dirty bookstore. I once saw a magazine in their magazine rack with a headline on the cover: "Cannibal Cocksuckers."

About half a block away on Romolo was the Basque Hotel and Restaurant. The hotel was a cheap boarding hotel, and the restaurant served a cheap, good, large fixed-price supper. I knew it by reputation, but the first time I went there, I was with a bunch of people – bridge players and kibitzers – who'd been drinking in the Coffee Gallery. There was a long line going from the bar to the entrance, and we decided to have a drink at the bar while we waited to be seated. The bartender said something about paying for the meal when we ordered our drinks, but the idea of paying for a meal before even being seated didn't sink in. We had a round and another and noticed people who'd come in after us were now being seated for supper. We decided we were too grungy and drunk for them and left in a huff. On the way out, one of the drunkest of us started yelling – three times before we made it to the door – "This isn't a real Basque Restaurant. This is just some kind of phony Basque Restaurant." It was months before I had the nerve to try again.

Right across from the Romolo apartment was a postage stamp-sized parking lot, with cars moving in and out – on weekends right up until the bars closed at 2 AM. Sometimes, a car alarm would get set off and sound over and over until it killed the battery. One time, an apartment dweller covered such a car with sticky chicken feathers. I appreciated the thought.

For a time, there was a crazy old Chinese woman in one of the apartments on Fresno Alley. She would be chanting in Chinese out the window at odd hours through the day and night. Some of the kids in the alley took to chanting Chinese-sounding gibberish back at her. She took it in good part, and she and the kids would keep up a sort of call and response chanting that they enjoyed much more than the tenants in the neighboring apartments.

Later, after Bill had sold the Coffee Gallery, he and Ellie moved on to Alaska leaving just me in the apartment. I had a couple roommates move in and out, neither lasting very long, then had it by myself when Candi moved in with me for a time. After she moved out, I was by myself again.

There were a number of people in the building I already knew from the bars.

Frank, the building manager, had the apartment right underneath. He was in his 60's. He made a little money as a street artist. San Francisco street artists were supposed to sell only things they made themselves, but Frank had hippie friends up North who made various things and used Frank as a sales outlet. They also grew some marijuana, and Frank also made a little from selling some of that for them. As building manager, his apartment was rent-free to him, and he would take a roommate and get a little more that way. All in all, he was comfortable enough.

Frank was a kind of father – or grandfather -- figure to Crystal Ball and some of her dancer friends, putting them up on his sofa from time to time. I recall one time Shirley, one of Frank's old friends, was visiting him, reminiscing about her life and how she had married the same man three times. Crystal, who was part of the group listening, showed her quirky common sense: "What was the matter?" she asked, "Couldn't you recognize him?"

Another time I came back to the building late at night to find a fire truck out in the alley and hoses pulled into the front of the building. The tenants were all out in the alley, watching what was happening. It didn't amount to much. There was no smoke to be seen, and nobody seemed excited. I saw Frank and asked him what was going on. "There was a little fire in the apartment across the hall from me," he said. "The firemen cleared the building, and everybody's out here now watching them mop up. Except Crystal. She's still finishing her makeup."

Toni Moves In

Toni lived with me in my apartment in Romolo alley for something like eight years. I don't remember exactly. Our time in that apartment came to an end twice, the second time for good. Neither of us decided that. My landlord did.

A lot of important things happened and didn't happen over that time. But the things that happened didn't lead to anything. The things that didn't, well, some were worse than what did, some better. You could feel the not happening things at the same time as the actual things, but not clearly. The potential things are like chambers in a mystery cavern hidden underneath you. You can sort of feel their presence, and it influences the imagination somehow, but you can't really say how exactly.

It was a little more than two months after Toni and I had suddenly become close that she moved in. After her second marriage broke up, she landed back in North Beach with no money and though she had deep ties in North Beach, neither she nor they were prepared for the sudden change in her fortunes. She had applied for a check for mental disability, but who knows how long something like that will take to decide? (I had a poet friend who had succeeded in getting mental disability. He said he regarded it as a kind of fellowship for the arts.) Toni immediately got behind in her rooming house rent. I had helped her with it once, a personal fellowship for the arts, but she remained broke.

Desperate, she went to her mother down the Peninsula, but they were old enemies from Toni's childhood. Mama kept patting herself on the back for her generosity in taking Toni in and gloating about what a mess Toni's life had come to. Toni visited

North Beach as often as she could, and on one of these, I told her she could move in with me until her disability came through.

She hadn't many choices, and between momma and me the decision was easy. It was awkward, though, because we were suddenly living in each other's laps before our relations were in any way settled, and Toni's life was still in an uproar. The second bedroom in the apartment had been a storage room, and it stayed that way. Toni took the living room couch as her bed and kept it that way all the time she lived with me there. It seemed a way to say that this was just a temporary arrangement. We never did settle into mutual routines. If we ate together, it was when, from time to time, I took her out for a meal.

I had a bunch of art on the walls and some sculptures.

My mother was an artist. Back when I was a small child she had taken adult education classes. She had learned mechanical sorts of drawing and painting techniques. Her first stuff was trite. As the years went by, she developed her individual tastes and skills. I had a little bit of my mother's stuff. One was a collage made not long before Toni moved in. It was made from pieces of paper painted with water colors then torn into scraps. It showed a female nude lying on her back, her hands clasped behind her head. It was quite voluptuous. Toni paid it a nice compliment: "Mothers don't do things like that."

One time, I had more or less accidentally visited Captain Marvelous's apartment above the Savoy Tivoli restaurant/bar. His apartment walls, even in the bathroom, were full of art, much of it from people in North Beach and some I had had no idea were artists. The Captain told me that he had had a fire in another apartment that had destroyed lots of what he then had and that he had rebuilt his collection over the years since. That the Captain, with all his affectations, turned out to have such an extensive collection and his own personal taste in art and that he'd exercised it over the years in building and then restoring a collection made a big impression on me.

The next year, at the Grant Avenue Street Fair, I saw a welded metal sculpture of a diver swimming through a school of fish. Each fish was individually made and welded to the next, and together, they formed a diagonally slanted figure eight. The diver was swimming in the opposite direction through the lower loop of the eight shape. The price tag was over $1,000. It had never before occurred to me to spend something like that for a piece of art. I circled around it through Saturday and decided that night that I couldn't pay $1,000, but I would still make an offer on it. Sunday morning, I went up to the artist and told him I was interested in buying Aquaflight. "Oh," he said casually, "Sorry. It's already sold." But I had got the bug and began to acquire stuff I liked here and there – including a couple pieces from that metal sculptor. Now Toni's stuff joined the other things on my walls, and my living room became her studio.

Toni and Andrew

Before Toni moved in with me, before we ever became close, she was in the midst of an affair with Andrew, a roofer -- in his late twenties at a guess. He'd been around North Beach three, four, or so years before Toni showed back up in the bars after her second marriage tanked. He was strong, quiet, intense, and younger. All of those were attractive to Toni then, and she was a trip in all kinds of ways for anybody. They were up and down, but all Toni's relationships were up and down. It didn't mean there wasn't a real bond. What Toni and I were or were to become was much less clear to any of us. She continued the affair with Andrew after moving in with me. When we had first become close, Toni had spontaneously confided in me about what was happening with Andrew, but she stopped that after she moved in, and she had the decency not to bring him around. It wasn't Toni's way to pause and figure things out. She went ahead in all directions.

When Toni first met him he had been shacked up with Cindy, one of Toni's street friends, the kind she warned me about: "Just because I talk to them doesn't mean you can trust them." Whether you could trust her or not, Cindy had a personality. I had run into her on the street one time on the way back from an Apple MacIntosh Users Group meeting. "Where you been?" she asked me. I told her. She perked up. "Apple MacIntosh? What's that? I never heard of that one before." I could tell she thought it was a new drug.

"Andrew," Cindy had said when she came back to her apartment and discovered Toni and Andrew in bed, "This wasn't in the brochure." This story had the same ring to me as the one Toni later told me about how she and Jerry C. had first gotten together.

I was younger than she but from the first Toni had told me, "You're too old for me." Nevertheless, it seemed to waver as to whether we might become lovers. At length, she seemed to have placed me as an odd sort of father figure. It wasn't what I wanted at all, and she knew it, but it was the best solution she could come to right then. She relied on me and rebelled against having to do so. She confided some things and hid others. We talked intimately and comfortably at times and about some things but then not at other times or about other things, and where the boundaries were, was never really clear. We were close, but no cigar.

Big Will and some of the other artists at Project Artaud had a show together. I took Toni, and beforehand took Toni to Big Will's studio/living space at Artaud to introduce her. She checked out his ceramic beads and big abstract acrylics. The paint was often dripped on, and the drops manipulated by tilting the canvas. Sometimes he brushed it on. But, however the paint got on, the shapes made were always vaguely like something, though you couldn't tell quite what. He was an artist after Toni's heart and a fine story-teller to boot, though his stories generally had a large amount of mystical bullshit mixed in.

For the show, Big Will had taken wood scraps in odd shapes (probably left overs from some other Artaud artist's work), painted them with glossy paints in bright multi-colored chaos, and glued them together into weird structures that looked something like grounded mobiles.

I think I was the only one wearing a watch in the place, and there were wall clocks nowhere. Time was obsolete.

There was a musical invention on display. Somebody had taken a hollow metal sphere with a rim around the center and a semi-circular hole in the sphere above the rim. It looked as if it had started life as some sort of mechanical part. There were metal strips of different lengths welded around the rim, each ending with a welded glob. A mic had been hooked up, hanging just into the hole in the sphere. There was a small hammer with a rubber tip like the one a nurse uses to test your knee-jerk reflex. You hit the tip of the strips with the hammer, and the mic picked up the vibrations as they sounded inside the sphere. Different length strips made different sounds. I was modestly high from the refreshments Big Will had given us and was fascinated with this instrument. I had taken the hammer, and it seemed to me as if I had become the

Mozart of this new sound. But Toni came over and took the hammer away from me. They had a band there that was getting ready to play.

Another time, I went with Toni to see one man <u>The Tempest</u> performed by Fred Curchack. Miranda was played by a big old-fashioned baby doll. She had a canvas sack for a torso and a big china face with eyes that clicked open and shut as you tilted her and rubber arms and legs. Both Prospero and Ferdinand treated her with the gentleness that such a beautiful young innocent deserved.

Curchack had a real gift for making the poetry of the play come alive. But what really made it stand out was his physical training and showmanship. He used shadow puppetry – moving behind a screen and playing with the shadows he created there. For the very end, Curchack as Prospero moved behind the screen. His shadow seemed to float up and disappear into thin air. He also introduced what the program said was Mongolian toning into the show. The toning seemed to hit some hidden chord in Toni that she hadn't known was there. It would have pretty much passed me by, except that I got a taste from Toni's reaction.

Another time, we went to see the movie <u>Ran</u> together, Kurosawa's adaptation of <u>King Lear</u>. There's a lot of high-intensity shouting in it, and one of the evil sisters had a particularly high-pitched shriek. Toni had gotten a gizmo that fits on her keychain to help her find her keys. You whistled, and the gizmo went, "Beep, beep, beep, beep." It responded to the shouting and shrieking. We tried sitting on the keychain, but it wasn't enough to muffle it. It was ridiculous, but we couldn't very well leave her keys at the concession counter.

These were the sorts of good times we had here and there.

Andrew went back East to see family. He was gone one month, then two, then called Toni to tell her he was coming back to North Beach. Toni hated talking on the phone and limited all her calls to the minimum time necessary. His call delighted her. She assumed he was coming back to pick up their affair where it had left off. He didn't tell her on the phone, but he was coming back to say good-bye.

Andrew's life in North Beach had been going nowhere but the bars. Roofing was steady work but exhausting and wasn't leading to anything except, as I say, to the bars. He parked his pick-up truck on the street, and homeless people would climb in the back to sleep. Sometimes, if he recognized the person, he'd let them be. Others he'd roust. Either way it was a nuisance and depressing. His partner Jeb was a semi-dependable, good-natured guy, but after a few drinks in the bar, he'd start intermittently shouting unintelligible phrases to nobody in particular. Firebird's favorite line at those times was, "Anybody who can understand Jeb is 86'd."

Andrew's parents and older brother had a family business. There had been some estrangement when Andrew left for San Francisco, but it wasn't deep. Now, they wanted him to come back and join the business. It was irresistible. A clear and promising new start with a family he loved instead of a tangled and frustrating life that felt too much like quicksand.

I suppose he couldn't bring himself to tell Toni on the phone that his coming back was a good-bye visit. As I say, heart-to-heart talks on the phone with Toni were not possible. And I suppose he partly wanted, partly felt obligated to wind it up with her in person. But there was no good way to break it to her. She was devastated.

Toni had done a collage once from slick magazine ads. It showed a lovely middle-class kitchen right out of a 50's TV sit-com. A lovely sit-com mama stood in the middle of it. But she had pushed the refrigerator until it blocked the kitchen door. The refrigerator door had a bulls-eye stuck on it. In the center of the bulls-eye, there was the head of a lovely, wise, middle-class sitcom husband. Mama was throwing darts at the bulls-eye. Toni couldn't imagine her Andrew choosing middle-class life over an affair with her.

I had hoped Andrew's departure might clear the way for me, but that didn't happen. As I've said, Toni seemed to have cast me as a sort of father, by definition, too old for her. She wanted to replace Andrew with another young stud. She was still a sexy woman, but hers was a tough life for anybody to want into.

Things Get Better Then Worse

Still, as Christmas season approached that year, things seemed to be getting better.

Ed and Jennie had invited us to a Christmas party. They were now living out in the Mission. They had started a business hauling junk for people who wanted to get rid of it. They sorted through the stuff afterwards and had a little thrift store where they sold the stuff that was salvageable. Sometimes, Small brought them stuff on consignment that she'd found in her dumpster diving. Their lives seemed to have come together; and, in fact, they had become one of the not very many successful couples in North Beach.

Toni told me that she had been a Universal Life minister and had married Jennie to her first husband, Indian Joe. Jennie also had Indian blood in her – in fact, her mother got a small tribal check – but the marriage was terrible. Indian Joe stayed drunk and hit her lots. Jennie supported them cocktail waitressing, making macramé, and cleaning houses. Finally, after two kids, she ditched him. I told Toni she could have been sued for malpractice for that marriage. She defended herself: "It was a great ceremony. Just the wrong people." Ed was a quiet guy who I knew from the bridge table at the Coffee Gallery. I never knew just how he got his money. He never had much but seemed to have barely enough. Before Jennie, he had taken on Marcie, a cocktail waitress at the Coffee Gallery who had been going with one of the bartenders. Then, all of a sudden, Marcie flipped out. She broke up with the bartender and seemed just to go into a funk. She stopped coming to work, and you could see her sitting on the street corners doing nothing. Ed had tried to get to her, to get her back into this world; but it didn't happen. Then he started up with Jennie, and that worked.

Now Toni got into the spirit for their Christmas party. She had shoes and shoes and shoes that she'd collected here and there along the way. I told her she had been a centipede in another life. She took a black pair of heels and used her acrylics to paint them a bright holiday red. She took a pair of black net panty hose, cut the feet off, cut a hole in the crotch, and made a top out of it. Bright red lipstick and some fake holly stuck in her hair.

Lots of North Beach people at the party. Garcia turned up. Toni and I never had the same opinion about him at the same time. He had a big ego but also some flair. Toni would tell me, "Garcia's an asshole." I would say, "I know he does act that way a lot, but he's ok." Gradually she'd convince me he's an asshole. But by the time she'd convinced me, Toni had changed her mind. "Garcia's an asshole," I'd say. "No, not really," she'd say, "He just acts like one."

Garcia played the guitar now and then at the Coffee Gallery. For this party, he showed up, held up his guitar case, and said, "I've got my guitar in here, and I've got a .45. Which would you rather hear?"

The vote went for the guitar. Garcia took it out and played some traditional Christmas music: "Jingle Bell Rock." A good time was had by all.

Alice Tall was at the party and offered us a ride back to North Beach, and we, all unknowing, accepted it. That was how I learned not to get in a car with her driving. Thank god it was the small hours, and the streets were empty. She could just barely keep it on the road as it was. I asked her to stop and let us out, but she thought I was joking and just kept swerving merrily along, singing and giggling.

Elmer's Glue was one of the staples of Toni's artistic life. She swore by it. It was what she used to stick everything together in her collages. That Christmas, I bought her a half-gallon bottle of Elmer's Glue. She thought it was funny, and she liked it. Then, one night soon afterwards I came out of my bedroom to use the bathroom and saw Toni, on speed, crying tears of anger, the glue bottle on its side, and she, in only panties and socks, standing in the middle of a big puddle of glue, which was just starting to spread to the collage she'd been working on. I rescued the collage as best I could. "Toni," I said, "You really stick to your art." She started giggling through her rage. For 15 minutes or so, I possessed perhaps the world's only living human collage.

Things seemed to be turning better, but it was precarious. I painfully recall one time when what started as an intimate moment turned bad. I can't recall any more just what the lead-up was. Toni and I were nearly naked. Everything was promising, but somehow we detoured off into a quarrel. In it I found myself saying, "All you women think you're sitting on a gold mine." Another time Toni herself had said something sort of similar. "As long as I've got one of these (pointing at her pussy), I can get all of those I want (pointing at my crotch)." But she said it in fun. When I said it in anger, she was furious. She pounded her right fist over her left breast, over her heart, and yelled at me, "This is my gold mine." It was true, and I was shamed, though not shamed enough to admit it at the time.

Toni's heart was loaded with immediacy of feeling, intuition, and a natural intimacy. In a conflicted world, that meant she took all the conflicts around her into that heart. She, as she said herself, was the original do/don't girl. She was never on just one side of any conflict. Gold mines can be dangerous places.

This quarrel spoiling something good sounds like a sort of train wreck. It wasn't.

I think a deep link between two people depends rather on a mutual instinct, each for the other, than on perfect understanding. It isn't even necessary for this instinct to be right as long as it is alive. In fact, where instinct overrides common sense and courtesy, it even promotes misunderstandings. I'll quote you a trivial example from Nadezhda Mandelstam's beautiful memoir of her marriage to Russian poet Osip Mandelstam. He would dictate his work to her:

"Before each session, he often went out walking for an hour or even two. When he returned, he was tense and bad-tempered, ordering me to sharpen my pencils and start work at once. The first few phrases he dictated so quickly, as though he remembered them by heart, that I could scarcely keep up with him. Later the pace slowed down, but I often got confused by the long sentences. He just failed to understand why I couldn't get them down at one go, but at the same time, I often found him leaving out one or even several words, as though he thought I could hear them without his actually having to utter them. 'Can't you see that it doesn't hang together without that?' he would ask impatiently. 'Do you think,' I snapped back at him, 'that I'm sitting in your head reading your thoughts? … Fool, fool, fool.' He got really angry at the word 'fool' and called me an idiot in return. I shrieked with rage, and he defended himself by saying that 'idiot' was a beautiful Ancient Greek word. So I was an ancient Greek fool into the bargain."

Silly spats like these, which are grounded in a complete confidence that they make no difference at all to the underleying connection, are more like a demonstration of the instinct underneath than a quarrel. In a way, they are almost like a kiss. Especially if you like spicy, hot, sweet and sour.

As I say, I think the underlying instinct depends rather on being alive than on understanding. It is this life that creates both understanding and misunderstanding. With good faith, it can be a game like a cat chasing its tail. But life is always going in different directions, and faith has to run to keep up.

Toni and I made peace, but the instinct between us was like an underground river. You could sense its presence but not reach into the water.

Good-bye Romolo

It was something external that brought things to a head.

I didn't grow up to be a good housekeeper. I had a messy room as a kid. When I moved into an apartment in Chicago with other college students, that apartment had the kind of funky sloppiness that such apartments often have. My time in Mississippi, North Carolina, and Jersey City did nothing for habits of neatness. The die was already cast before I ever came to San Francisco.

Toni's coming sort of doubled down on the mess already there. Take the kitchen, for example. It didn't get used much for cooking. I had long ago gotten into the habit of eating my meals in the cheap restaurants around North Beach and Chinatown. What and how Toni ate, I'm not really sure, but whatever it was, she didn't cook to speak of. Instead, Toni was more likely to be melting colored plastic on one of the stove burners for use in a mask. The apartment door happened to be open one day, and my landlord, passing by, happened to get a look inside. He immediately ordered us to get out. I got some advice from a tenant's rights group and negotiated a bit with the landlord's lawyer. We made a deal. Toni would leave, and I would paint the apartment, and I would stay.

Toni didn't complain. She didn't have much to say at all about the whole situation. She had long ago gotten her disability check, so she was poor but not entirely destitute. For myself, I wasn't interested to find a new place with Toni to prolong the odd sort of life we'd had together at Romolo.

I didn't know exactly what arrangements Toni made, and I didn't see much of her around the bars. Grace, who had been our neighbor across the hall at Romolo, had quite a while back moved to a different apartment; and, as I later learned, Toni moved in with her and her daughter for a while. But Toni couldn't live in a place without taking it over, and Grace finally told Toni she'd have to move out. Toni couldn't find another place. After Romolo, Grace had briefly lived in a room above the Saloon. When she took a new apartment, she kept the room above the Saloon for storage. She, at length, gave Toni a key to that room so at least she'd have a place to sleep while she looked for something else. Toni was there for months until the fire.

I don't remember all the details now. I never saw the fire itself. Even the fire trucks were gone by the time I got on the scene. The fire had started in the rooms above the Saloon. It wasn't a complete disaster, but enough to close down the bar for repairs for a month or so. There hadn't been that many people living in the rooms at that time, but they all had to move out for the repairs. Some people were saying the fire was Toni's fault. I have no way of knowing for sure, but I don't believe it myself. Toni told me later she had been in Grace's room, had been startled, turned around to the window and saw fire coming in the window. The shock had paralyzed her for a moment before she came to and got the hell out. It seemed to me, looking at that window from the outside of the building, that I could see char marks as if a flame had entered there. But nobody had a clear account of what happened, and the crowd living there was a careless bunch. Toni, of course, heard the rumors that she was somehow to blame, and it hurt her a lot when she was already down.

When I arrived on the scene Toni was one of the crowd standing outside looking at the damage. There was nothing else for it. I took her back to the Romolo apartment with me. She was now contraband there, of course, but as long as the landlord didn't happen to spot her, nobody in the building was going to say anything.

It was after she moved back in that Toni lost her teeth. From the time we first became close, she was really long in the tooth. I don't think I ever saw a toothbrush of hers in all the years at Romolo. Her gums were in terrible shape. It came to a crisis, and all her teeth had to come out. She was on Medi-Cal, the California welfare medical program, and it covered the extractions, and it also covered dentures. But Medi-Cal dentures were the cheapest of the cheap. And the dentists who took Medi-Cal were lots of them guys who concentrated on quantity, not individualized care. The dentures were not a great fit, and often, she didn't wear the lowers. Toni didn't talk about it, but besides being uncomfortable, they didn't do anything for her ego.

It all made me think of a chain gang song I learned during my activist days:

> "The Captain, he kept me in cast iron shackles.
> The Captain, he kept me in cast iron shackles.
> It hurts my legs, Lord, it hurts my legs.
>
> The Captain, he fed me grits and 'lasses.
> The Captain, he fed me grits and 'lasses.
> It hurts my pride, Lord, it hurts my pride."

Then, I took a vacation to Brazil. I had gone to see the movie
<u>Kiss of the Spiderwoman</u> with Tall and a couple of her friends. I
didn't know anything about it and was expecting some kind of
Grade C horror flick. Instead, I got a beautiful movie, and in the
credits, I noticed "Sugarloaf Productions". And that made me think
of one of my all-time favorite movies, <u>Black Orpheus,</u> set in Rio
during Carneval. And that made me think of another favorite, <u>Bye
Bye Brazil</u>. These were each so beautiful in the photography and
the story so moving in a direct and simple way, that I became
inspired to make a vacation trip to Brazil. I saw three cities: Rio,
Manaus, and Salvador, and I had a great time. I brought gifts back
for Toni, Tall, and Candi. The gifts for Candi and Tall I picked up
at a street fair in Rio: a hash pipe for Tall and earrings for Candi.
(The black customs lady checking me through at the airport when I
returned gave me a knowing half-smile as she examined the hash
pipe.) Candi's earrings were dragons cut from a sheet of copper,
just thick enough not to be fragile. They had been stamped to give
them scales and an oval for an eye. Toni took an interest in knives.
In Manaus, way up the Amazon, at a tourist stop at an Indian
village, I saw a knife with big porcupine quills decorating the
handle. I got that for Toni.

Toni didn't like the knife. She laughed at it – "a hairy knife."
Instead, she liked the earrings I'd gotten for Candi, and she
appropriated them for herself. I told her I'd get her other earrings
or whatever instead of the knife but that those earrings from Brazil
were for Candi. But Toni had decided, "I like these," and she
wouldn't surrender them.

I had seen before, and I had it brought home to me now, that
even when somebody refuses you romantically, that doesn't

prevent them from being jealous when you pay attention to somebody else. I've even noticed that sort of feeling in myself when I'd seen somebody I knew was attracted to me turn their attention to someone else. It's not really logical but anybody who thinks only the logical is real is living in a fantasy world. I talked to Tall and asked her to talk to Toni to see if she could get her to give the earrings back. Tall was too smart for that. "I'm not stepping into that one, honey." I eventually saw them lying around the apartment, expropriated them, and gave them to Candi. Toni, of course, was mad, but it didn't really make our relations any worse.

My brother visited San Francisco, and I put him up for three or four days. Toni very generously vacated the living room couch for him while she slept in the storage room bedroom.

My brother later told me of a conversation he overheard one night when Toni brought Terrible Tommy back to the apartment with her after the bars closed. They talked in near whispers in the kitchen, thinking my brother was asleep. But he wasn't.

I can think of three, maybe four, Terrible Tommy's that I knew in North Beach over the years. "Tommy" just goes too naturally with "Terrible." It's like a fate determined when they put the little name bracelet on the newborn.

Tommy told Toni he had some heroin and wanted her to have some. "No," she said, "I'm just a little person. It would kill me."

"O, that's alright, Toni. I don't mind. I want you to have it."

"No, it would kill me."

Tommy was really fucked up. "Toni, I love you. It's alright. I want to give it to you."

"You're sweet, but it would kill me."

And on and on.

And so our life went on and on. Until my landlord caught sight of Toni again and threw us both out. This time, there was no negotiating.

I had arrived in North Beach at a loss. There, without my direct setting about to create it, I gradually grew a new life inside and out. Toni popped into it. Life with her was unexpected in so many ways. It was a reality I could never have imagined or wished for on my own. It was like a test to which the answer book had been lost before the questions were even written. In the end external circumstances brought it to an end, and yet they didn't. One way and another, Toni and I came back together and apart and together until her death. And then she came back again. It was all full of frustrations both sides, and yet, if I were ever given a choice to erase the whole thing out of my life, I would take every part of it without even blinking.

. It was like Bottom's dream but with the pilot's voice telling you, "We are experiencing turbulence. Fasten your seat belts.". Dreams are powerful, and there is more to them than we can recollect or formulate. Recalling and making sense of them, it seems to me, is sort of like dragging a mermaid ashore. Of course we have to pay the rent and taxes and so forth, but is that all there is? We only very partially get to choose how things turn out. The richness of life is not in having things turn out the way we want but what is inside the experience. There, I got a gold mine.

CHAPTER 10 TONI'S OPPORTUNITY MASK

As I've said, Small was a genius dumpster diver. One day, she showed up at the Broadway apartment with something she'd found in a bin beside a thrift shop in the Mission. It was a sort of coffee table whose base was a real elephant's foot. She recognized it right off as the kind of freakish thing Toni would go for and had latched on to it as a gift to patch up the tension between them. Toni was looking at it speculatively when I carelessly said to Toni, "Pretty much like your Opportunity Mask."

"Like my Opportunity Mask? What do you mean?"

"O, nothing. Just something in a dream I had."

"Tell me about it."

Now, I was sorry I had let that slip out. I had no idea where that dream might lead to and, frankly, was a little afraid to find out.

"It was just something in a dream. I don't remember it very well."

"Just tell me what you remember. It sounds interesting."

"Well, ok. It was after you died. In my dream, I started hearing neighborhood rumors that you were back around again. "That can't be," I'd say, "She's dead." Still, every now and then, someone would say, "I hear Toni's back." Then, one afternoon, I walked into one of the bars, and there you were behind it. You didn't look great, but there you were.

'What are you doing here?' I asked, 'You're dead.' You just said, 'Blah, blah, blah, blah, blah, blah...'"

"Then, a day or two later, a guy showed up at my door. He said he was a friend of yours, and you had told him he could have your Opportunity Mask, and you told him just to tell me to give it to him."

'First of all,' I told him, 'Toni left everything scattered all over everywhere in a complete mess. Second of all, I don't know what you're talking about.'

'You know, her Opportunity Mask.'

'It's not really just a mask. It's really a multi-Medea, I mean Media, sculpture. You know. The elephant with the feathers.'

"Then I did vaguely remember it, but not very well, and I still didn't know what had become of it."

As I'd feared she didn't seem to like my dream encounter with the guy who came to pick up the mask and was clouding over more when I went on to tell her about how the dream continued in a lawyer's office. I was afraid I was in for a thunderstorm. But she kept thinking about it and began clearing some. "But it shows you really were in touch with me even though you didn't understand it," she said. "You think you're so scientific, but you're not. I don't know how anybody so stupid could be so intelligent and vice versa." She thought some more. "I bet the guy was young and looked like a biker. You were just jealous."

Toni liked bikers. Mostly, they had strong, simple emotions. Toni's were at once simple and complex, so she had a two-to-one edge on them. When she felt in control she was generous, so the relationships worked out well.

Now, she was a little pleased with herself and gave me a mild slap upside the head. I was happy to get off so easy.

"Then the dream shifted to a lawyer's office. I was explaining to him that, first of all, you were dead. Second, you were always putting stuff in storage, then losing it when you couldn't keep up with the payments, or losing it some other way; and I had looked through the stuff of yours I had, and it wasn't there. Then I looked over in the comer and saw you sitting there on the floor, with your back half turned, throwing Tarot cards. I pointed you out to the lawyer, but he couldn't see you. 'You're hallucinating,' he said. Then I woke up."

A lawyer's office is like a dry cough you can't get rid of. I sort of envied Toni sitting on the floor, wrapped in a personal mysticism but still a presence at the center of what was going on.

Toni thought about my dream for a minute or two. "Shame on you for all that negative stuff," Toni said. "But you were upset. I guess it's ok. But tell me what the Opportunity Mask looked like."

"Well, it's not a mask in the regular sense but a sculpture maybe four feet high. Brightly colored paper mache like some Mexican pieces I've seen – sort of a full body mask – or a piñata."

"You know Ganesha, the Indian elephant god? I once saw a Japanese print of him in sexual union with a beautiful woman. The print was labeled "The Lord of Obstacle." A friend who had done business in India had explained to me some months before my dream, 'Ganesha is 'The Lord of Obstacle' in the same sense as St. Jude is the saint of lost causes.' The head of the mask is Ganesha's head."

"Wow, Lord of Obstacle," she said. "I've seen those elephant pictures before, but I didn't know anything about that. Go on about what it looked like."

"The body is a naked full-breasted Hindu dancer's body. The arms are gesturing in the dance. One foot is lifted. The skin is a dark tone. The pussy is a bright red-orange, like an elliptical vertical bullseye. There are deep purple and bright black concentric circles around it, blending gradually into the overall dusky flesh tone. On the outside of one breast is your Madonna I image, and on the other one Madonna III. The same images appear, but on opposite sides, on the cheeks of the ass. There are large slightly splayed fingers and toes with big red colored nails. When you look more closely, you realize that these are really tiny elephant feet that just look like fingers and toes. Toward the back of either shoulder, there is a macaw's face tatoo. Out of the back, a big pair of red and gold macaw's wings come out."

Toni thought about it for a moment. "Wow," she said. "That's something else. Even though this is just coming at me now, it's almost like I dreamed it in you. I mean, what you got is right, a lot of it, but I don't think some of the details are right about how he looked. But the wings are right. If a god wanted to fly, he could; and, if he could, he would, so he'd need wings."

Toni had me doing research on Ganesha for her – finding pictures on the internet, and finding Ganesha stories.. She had the pictures spread out on a table in the apartment the way she would do when she was working on a collage and trying to nudge her imagination how to fit them together. At length she started on it.

She already had the real elephant foot from Small's gift. The other foot came from a mannequin. She put a ballet slipper on it "because Ganesha was a dancer," and she glued a red high heel onto the slipper. "Because high heels are sexy, and sex is an opportunity. But even when it's good, you don't really know if it's a good opportunity or not, and even if it is good, it seems like there's always something in the way, so that's why you need Ganesha, the Lord of Obstacle."

Her comment set off a train of association in me. What about men who like sex but not personal intimacy? It's not so very uncommon. The Duke, for example, liked sex as well as anybody. He liked to spend money, joke around, and get laid but scarcely cared to know names. He told me once about a time at the crap house a woman who thought she was his old lady started to hit on him. "Of course, it was because I was drunk and spending. I told her, 'Get away from me woman, because I don't chew my tobacco twice.'"

My friend Mel, the ex-merchant marine, had a similar attitude. He'd married a Japanese woman and brought her to the States, but it didn't work out. He told me, "I couldn't wait to ship out, get away from my wife, and see the whores in the ports, my loved ones." The easy familiarity of the bars was where he was at home. He had no intention of opening the doors to his inner life.

Another time, I was in Frank's apartment, who lived downstairs from me at Romolo. I've mentioned how he used to put up Crystal Ball every now and then when she was between boyfriends or feuding with one. On this occasion, he had a Korean woman friend visiting him. She was talking about how she'd lived in Turkey for a while and had a lover who was a drug dealer. He got busted and sent to prison for a long sentence. "It was pure sex," she said, "but you just can't fuck somebody for 8 years without feeling a little something for them." She sounded a little disappointed in herself for this weakness. But I said to myself, "This is the back door of love, opened by its closing."

I told Toni, "For a lot of people, sex isn't so much. It's just getting laid."

Toni dismissed that, "Yeah, there are a lot of assholes in this world. I know a biker; he brags about what a great old lady he has 'because she can really take a punch.'"

Usually, Toni did everything herself in her artwork, but this time, she enlisted help. She got Mary Thomas, the old near-sighted ex-stripper who lived above the Saloon, to sew the body. Mary, despite being extremely near-sighted, had a talent for intricate, detailed craft projects. For example, she made tiny dollhouses from kits. One Halloween, she had sewed me a Rainier Ale cape. She used shiny green, gold, and red satin, matching the colors on the bottles. She studied how the red "R" on the label was done with great care and reproduced it with great fidelity. I wore it on Halloween with great success, then later on my birthday wore just the cape, a pair of boxer shorts, and a pair of slippers down to the 6 AM shift at Gullivers. I was a big hit, and I decided to go across the street to the Saloon, but Lena, who then had the early morning shift there, wouldn't serve me. "I've known you for a long time, Bob," she said, "but I can't serve you unless you put your shorts on."

"Alright," I said, "Where are they?"

"On your head, you asshole. Who put them there?"

"O, that. That was Firebird," I said and put my shorts back in their normal place.

The cape was before Toni and I became close, but afterward, she resurrected it to make me another Halloween costume, a sort of

Merlin outfit featuring a wand and a kind of magician's hat with a star-spangled computer floppy disk stuck in front.

Anyhow, Toni got Mary Thomas to sew Ganesha's head and body. She used heavy grey canvas and some grey suede for the ears. There were shiny silver buttons for the eyes. The face had a half smile that could go either funny or sad, one of Toni's habitual expressions. Toni half-drove Mary crazy getting that right.

Toni made me go to a pet shop that had macaws and get macaw feathers for her for the wings. After Toni died, I got a couple Huichol Indian pieces: one a jaguar head, the other a mask of a face. These are made with tiny brightly colored beads in various bright colors. The beads are stuck onto a wooden base that's been covered with beeswax. There must be thousands of beads in a mask only six inches or so high. These Indians use peyote in their rituals, and you could tell it from these exotic visionary masks.

Toni really liked them. She decided to make one of her own and put it in Ganesha's belly. She found some very small cheap plastic beads and spattered them with acrylic paints in the basic colors she wanted – red, blue, white, yellow, orange, green, black – and just a touch of metallic in silver and gold. She painted the mask design she wanted, then meticulously pasted the beads onto the belly to match the painting.

"The mask in the belly is a third eye. Because he's a dancer, and your balance is in your belly. What you see with just your head is like just one eye. No depth. No feel. You have to see from your gut, too."

The head, trunk, and body were stuffed with cut-up scraps from some of my clothes and Toni's. Toni had wanted to put candy hearts in also, but I pointed out that those would draw bugs. So she found some small red heart-shaped bracelet charms, got me to buy a package, and mixed them into the stuffing. "This is not just what you see on the outside," she said. "The inside has to be right, too."

When it was finished, Toni had it sitting in the apartment and would study it from time to time, not completely sure whether it was really done. Was there anything else needed? Anything that wasn't right? "I'm just not sure if it's really worthy yet," she would say. She was doing that one night and suddenly started giggling, then a full-throated laugh. "What's so funny?" She pointed at Ganesha. "What's the matter with you?" she said, "You must be blind. It's the elephant in the room between us." She found a Rainier Ale can in the kitchen wastebasket, took a pair of heavy kitchen shears, cut out just the word "Rainier," and glued it onto the base of the Ganesha around in the back. "That's just between us," she says, "so I'm putting it there where most people won't even look at it."

She came over to me, sat down beside me, wrapped her tail around one of my ankles, pressed her flat titties against my chest, and kissed me. It was moments like this that made living with Toni sweet.

A lot of the early freedom had come back between us, and the reserves right now were friendly ones once again. Living with a Dakini all of a sudden, out of the blue was a real curve ball, but it was just like Toni to do something like that. After that one conversation with the Duke, I didn't even try to think it all through. I was trying to see it all through the eye in my gut.

The Opportunity Mask was about three feet high. Badges drilled a hole in the foot and weighted it with some lead so it would stand up without wobbling.

We had a little party to celebrate the completion of the Opportunity Mask. The Alice was there, Mary Thomas, and Badges. Toni had taken something, "Because when I look at his belly, I can't celebrate right if I'm straight."

It made me think of how, one time, one of Toni's friends had shared some drug with her. When it started to come on Toni had turned to her friend and said, "Wow, can you imagine what it would be like to feel like this all the time.?" Her friend had given Toni a puzzled look, then shrugged and said, "Like what?"

Anyhow, it was a good party. Small smoked a lot of grass and twittered out her pride in donating the elephant's foot base. "See that? I found that in the Mission and gave it to Toni. She started it all because of me. Look at the wings. I gave her an elephant that can fly."

Toni decided to show off the Opportunity Mask on the Limbo Shift. Badges nailed together a small platform about 16 inches high and covered it with a tarp. The Opportunity Mask sat on top of it in the back of the Saloon. It was roped off behind some chairs to protect it from damage. That night, Small had attended a poetry reading at the Grant and Green. Leon was there reading an ode to guns and the revolution. A big biker with the stars and stripes on his t-shirt liked the stuff about guns but not the stuff about revolution. Small started to argue with him. It became more a flirtation than an argument, and Small started to tell him about Toni and how Milarepa made her a Dakini and now she was tending bar at the Limbo Shift down at the Saloon. "And she made an elephant god mask because of the elephant table I got her," Small said. "It's down at the Saloon right now." The biker was a skeptic but decided to come along and see this elephant god.

Lately, everything had been mellow with Small and Toni, so Badges let Small and her biker in without any problem. Small was still going on about Toni and Milarepa and Ganesha. Jerry C. was playing his jazz. The bar was crowded so the biker couldn't easily push his way through for a drink. Was this scene for him?

"This Milarepa – I don't see why it's such a big deal," he said. "To me it's a pile of shit," he said. But he was rubbing the side of his face with his left hand as he said this as if he really had tried to understand but still didn't get it.

There was a neon sign on the wall – the yellow outline of an electric guitar with blinking red letters spelling "Budweiser" where the strings should be. When the biker called suchness a pile of shit, there was a loud electric pop and buzz from the sign. The outline of a little green man, cross-legged, holding the guitar across his lap appeared. Instead of the red "Budweiser," there appeared text, twinkling as it scrolled, white on black:

"That is the beginning of Enlightenment, the realization of an arhat. It needs completion. The Buddha is suchness. The Buddha is a dry shit stick. Suchness is very useful and very necessary. But Suchness is not light. Suchness is not dark. It is not success or failure. Suchness is not happiness or sadness. It is not a solution or dis-solution. It is the beating heart of compassion." With another electric buzz, Milarepa disappeared, and "Budweiser" reappeared.

The bar laughed. The biker thought it was some kind of weird practical joke on him, and he didn't like it. By this time, he had pushed his way up to the bar. Toni slapped him across the face with her tail. The biker hadn't really gotten a good look at Toni before. When she slapped him, his shoulders bulged for a moment as if ready to fight. Then Toni turned blue from her tail down, red from waist to shoulders, and with little white stars twinkling over her whole body, a living flag. The biker says, "Wow." She says, "That was your wake-up call." She poured the biker a double shot, then nodded to Jerry, who started to play again. Toni came from behind the bar to do her regular color dancing. The biker dropped backward onto a stool and just watched. Everything cool.

I talked to her about it later. "Yeah, I've been practicing that flag. What a great chance to use it. Bikers are rooty-poots. You just have to know how to punch their buttons." Toni could play them like a fiddle.

CHAPTER 11 TONI'S MADONNA

This seems like a natural place to talk about Toni, the artist, and, in particular, about her Madonna.

She told me her father had an artistic bent of some sort. As a small girl, Toni wanted to imitate him. She found some paint and went to work with it on the walls, anticipating as she painted the admiration she would win. Instead, she was punished. If her parents thought that would teach her not to do that, they didn't much know the do/don't girl born to them. Creative expression became the one unifying thread running through a life of all sorts of ups and downs.

She had been born right-handed, she told me, but rheumatic fever (I think that was what she said) had forced her to use her left as her dominant hand. She did ok that way, but you could tell she wasn't a natural lefty. Her signature, for example, was big and sprawling like a child's. I doubt she ever had any formal art instruction. She managed sort of like the Union Maid: "One day she got sick, she couldn't draw anymore. She said, 'I'll draw on anyhow.'" Her strength was in her ideas rather than in formal execution. Perhaps her handicaps in realistic representation even encouraged her fantasy. And I've always thought that her fondness for making collages had to do with the physical difficulty she had with drawing.

I also think Toni likely was pulled into visual art by the physicality of image-making. She brought her body right into her thinking. It was like her Tarot readings. She had to touch the cards and see them in the layouts for her intuitions to start working. The same, I think, with lovers.

In the same way, I would see her so many times trying out photos for collages in different positions against some background. "I love squares," she said to me once. And often, she'd start a collage with some sort of arrangement of squares – maybe checkerboard or squares overlapping in different sizes. Often she would draw or paint over the collage, either before or after she'd arranged the photos on it. One collage she told me she'd done at 13 had a photo of one of Rodin's erotic sculptures. Around and over it, she'd drawn in thick black lines a girl's face, sucking a cock. I told you her physicality was basic to her art.

In fact, she told me she had had a baby at eleven years old. "My parents told me not to kiss. They never told me not to fuck." Her parents had placed her in a home for unwed mothers until she delivered. The baby was immediately taken away for adoption. The delivery, Toni said, had gone smoothly. "It just came right out." The birth had been a sensual experience for her, but having the baby immediately taken away left her with a sense of incompleteness about the whole thing. It was like the spot where a tooth had come out that you keep touching with your tongue. She never said anything to me about what had happened to get her pregnant. The loss she talked about was her distress at having the baby taken away at being denied completion of the experience.

As to her overall education, I never did know just how far Toni got in school. My guess is that she never finished high school. I know she was underage when she first came to North Beach and took up with Jerry C. Just how much underage, I don't know. But having the baby would have kept her out of elementary school for a while, and, given her overall rebelliousness, it wouldn't surprise me if she had been held back a little along the way. But I really don't know.

For painting, acrylics were her favorite, and she really liked bright metallics. But she would use lots of things. For example, there was a painting done in India ink on heavy foil of blackbirds pecking for food with a big red sun rising behind them. It was done long before I met her and was an early gift she gave me. While she lived with me, she turned to using spray paints from the hardware store for some things. She was nothing if not versatile as to media. I've mentioned that, at one point; she took over my stove for melting colored plastic into strange suggestive shapes.

Her Madonna was a painting she did long before I even knew who she was. She always took it as her central work. I don't really know just when she did it. I'm guessing somewhere between Jerry C. and her second husband. She said she painted it in a kind of possession and that her mood and the painting freaked out the guy she was living with at the time. I don't know how long it took to complete. From seeing her at work on various things, I'm guessing about a week, give or take a couple days. There's an image of it below. It's an acrylic, about 27" tall by 20" wide. (Incidentally, I accidentally discovered that you could rotate the painting ninety degrees counterclockwise, and it views about equally well.)

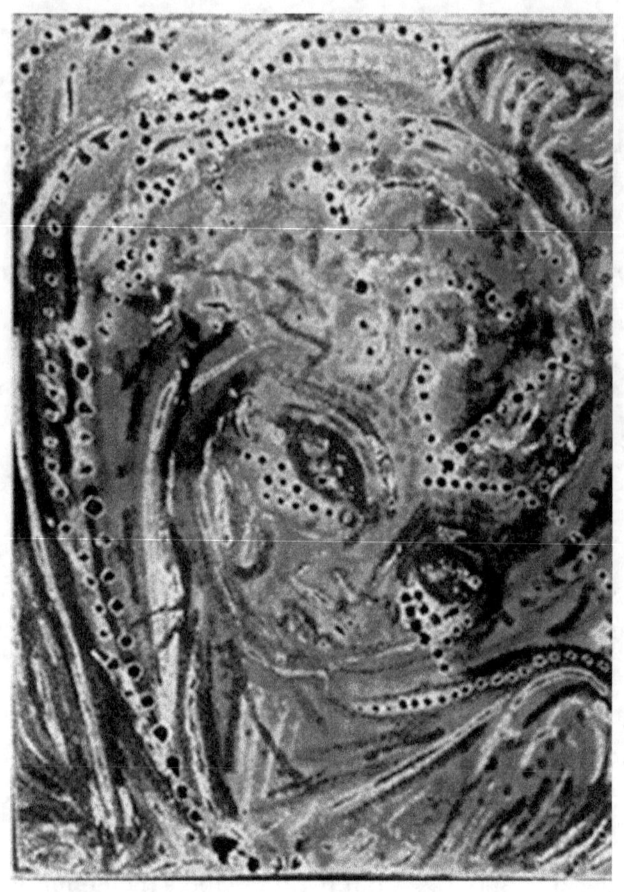

The colors are red, orange, black, white, some yellow and green. The style has something of a psychedelic quality in the way the natural qualities of the face are transformed, but the vision overall has a meditative, not mind-blowing quality. The colors are also not as sharp and bright as psychedelics often are.

When we first became close, and I visited her in the little room she had in a rooming house above a Columbus Avenue storefront, Madonna had pride of place on the wall. Later, after she moved in with me, it also took preeminence among the art on my walls.

Madonna had two successor paintings, both painted while she was living with me – the first one at the Romolo apartment, the other on Broadway.

The first I would never have recognized as related to Madonna if Toni hadn't said so. I didn't like it. It hadn't the Madonna face or figure, and it showed a pinched and narrow world. I took it to be a statement of a depressed mood. She talked to me some about it, and I sort of saw the Madonna relationship in her mind then, but I still didn't like it and didn't want to talk about it with her. I don't know what happened to it after she died.

Madonna III she painted during the brief time she, Grace, and I were living on Broadway. It was not on regular canvas but on a rough piece of cloth she found somewhere. She used black and red spray paint and some of her acrylics. Maybe she thought the rough cloth worked better than canvas with the spray paint, catching paint in droplets that hardened as they dried. It was a fcmale face with frizzed-out Afro-style hair. She had big eyes. I could see the relation to Madonna, but to me, this one was a case of the lights are on, but nobody's home. I was impressed with it as a painting, but it also was disturbing to me for what it hinted of Toni's mood. This one I still have.

Milarepa said, "Suchness is the beating heart of compassion."

Some people say compassion is feeling sorry for the troubles of others. Others say just feeling sorry isn't real compassion. You have to do something to cure the situation. Sometimes you can do something, sometimes you can't. Doing something isn't exactly the point either. People who are always curing others' troubles can be so smug. And with such complacent pride in their practical judgment of what can and can't be done and what other people should and shouldn't feel.

Compassion is spontaneous and natural and reaches out, as the Buddhists say, to all sentient beings.

I visited my friend Dolly a time or two at his home to watch ball games. His wife told me a story about their daughter when she was a small child. She had had a little pet turtle. The turtle stopped moving. The girl had heard that turtles hibernate, and she was convinced her turtle was hibernating. She put him in a plastic refrigerator dish and put him in the refrigerator. He kept hibernating. Finally, after more than a year had gone by, Dolly threw him out. His daughter took months to speak to him again. Even at the time when I heard the story, when his daughter was getting ready to go off to college, she had only barely forgiven him.

I suppose you could say her Madonna expressed Toni's religion, but really she was more a kind of free-form mystic than anything specific. Her beliefs had the quality of a dream you can't clearly remember except for how it moved you. If you try to tell it, to pin it down to something expressible, it loses in significance what it gains in clarity. Toni's art came directly out of her chaotic life. Did the art justify the chaos? I do/don't know, but I won't tell you unless you buy me a drink.

The heart beating in our body keeps our body alive. The heart of compassion keeps our humanity alive. "As in water face answereth to face, so the heart of man to man." (Proverbs 27:19). The image is fragile, never completely still, but it repairs itself when disturbed. It is this spontaneous and instinctive mirroring of ourselves in others, others in ourselves, sometimes comforting, sometimes troubling, that makes the depth of life possible. I imagine Toni's Madonna looking at her infant, who is maybe happy, maybe crying, but in neither case, knowing much beyond whether the titty is or isn't there. Mama knows the world and knows what a lot of. trouble the world holds for her son and for her. And still she smiles. Ecclesiastes 7:3 "Sorrow is better than laughter: for by the sadness of the countenance the heart is made better." There are some true smiles that dive deeper than laughter.

CHAPTER 12 YOUR CALL SOON

I've admitted this is not a straightforward story. The events have twists and turns, as does what happens to the people and inside the people. I'm sort of telling it from inside the Gordian knot.

What I have for you is an inside view, not simply of the events but also inside me as I puzzled through them. In a way, it's like Toni shuffling through her boxes of magazine photos, trying to get a collage to emerge from them.

Life doesn't move in straight lines. I had wanted to change the world and wound up in North Beach, where people weren't really into causes, even though some said they were. Instead, it was all about just figuring out how to live life and that at a very simple human level and with varying success. I recall a basically good-natured guy who always wore a cowboy hat. He killed himself jumping out the third-floor window from his cheap hotel room. Some people said he'd been so obnoxiously drunk that he got locked inside his room. He yelled, "You're never going to lock me in," and jumped out the window. Others said he wasn't locked in at all but just too stupid drunk to manage how the door sometimes stuck. Whatever -- a pointless way to leave this life. Others pulled themselves together in very individual ways, like my friends Alice Tall and Dolly. Toni, the do/don't girl, always teetered back and forth until she could come to some sort of unbalanced balance and put it into a mask or collage or painting or something.

This story is sort of realistic in that it starts with a tangled mess. A lot of things happen, and in the end, it's still a tangled mess. But realism by itself has no life in it, no spirit. And this story, as you've seen, has a lot of spirits in it trying to speak to you.

CHAPTER 13 THE FUTURE OF THE LIMBO SHIFT

I didn't see how the Limbo Shift could go on. It had crashed once over the incident with Small, Adam, and the asshole. Toni had been able to get around that one, but only barely. She'd been able to save the incident with the biker and the Opportunity Mask before anything happened, but it had been close. Even though she ran it irregularly and just now and then, it was completely illegal, and gradually, more and more people heard about it, and there would be more trickling in, even though she and Badges tried to be careful. It was just too unstable. There was bound to be a crash somehow.

One weekend morning, Alice Tall was filling in for Firebird's morning shift. When the shift was over, she invited me up to the Crow's Nest to share a joint. Small was out. It was just us. We settled ourselves in the window, looking out over Columbus and Broadway. While she rolled, I started talking about my worries about the Limbo Shift. She didn't say anything. Just rolled. She lit the joint, took a toke, and passed it to me. I took my toke and passed it back. I let out my breath but didn't say anything. The joint came back to me. Tall finally just said, "Toni always does it her way. She always has. With everybody." And that was all the talk we had. We finished the joint and just sat there staring out at the street for a little bit. "Well, thanks," I said. "I guess I should get on my way."

And things just went on. I just simmered inwardly. But that was nothing new for me. Then, one night, I had a dream.

There was a big event in Washington Square Park. A big crowd and a stage and sound equipment set up.

Then Dick Gregory, the great black comedian and activist, came out on the stage. He was just coming off of one of his hunger strikes. He was skin and bones, and his face had sunken in on itself. He walked slowly, every step an effort.

I looked around the crowd. Bob Kaufman was there, strikingly dressed as he sometimes was. Big velvet hat. A red cape. He even had a kid's wooden sword. The awful poet William Wadsworth was there. A kind of cartoon character, although he was completely unaware of it. He was maybe 60 or so, a widower who liked to try his luck hitting on attractive young women with some of the most ridiculous come-on lines in the world. For example, "Would you like to come up to my hotel room and talk about Mildred (his long-dead wife)?" Behind his back, everybody called him Willie World's Worst. Candi was over a little ways from me talking to some guy. She had Toni's Dakini tail, though nobody was paying any attention to it. Toni was over a little way in the other direction talking to Andrew. She was wearing Candi's dragon earrings, the gift I had brought back from Brazil for Candi and that had caused such a ruckus when Toni had appropriated them for herself.

The stage set was a bar scene. It was the Boar's Head Tavern in Eastcheap. Gregory was playing Falstaff. He stuffed a bunch of pillows into the jacket he had on to make himself fat, but he just looked weird. I saw My Lord Chief Justice come down off the stage and walk through the crowd, taking pictures of people with his smartphone. He had a sort of phosphorescent gleam in his eyes, no doubt thinking of how many of them he could arrest later. Then Gregory began delivering my very favorite speech. Prince Hal had been called back to his father, Henry IV, to account for his dissolute ways. The Pince and Falstaff were role-playing. Hal had just acted out his father reproaching him for his low company and especially that old villain Falstaff. Now it is Falstaff's turn, acting out the Prince's reply. Gregory's voice, at once hollow and booming, says:

> If sack and sugar be a fault, God help the wicked! If to be old and merry be a sin, then many an old host that I know is damned: if to be fat be to be hated, then Pharaoh's lean kine are to be loved. No, my good lord; banish Peto, banish Bardolph, banish Poins: but for sweet Jack Falstaff, kind Jack Falstaff, true Jack Falstaff, valiant Jack Falstaff, and therefore more valiant, being, as he is, old Jack Falstaff, banish not him thy Harry's company, banish not him thy Harry's company: banish plump Jack, and banish all the world.

The Grateful Dead broke into their number, "What a long, strange trip it's been."

I woke up. I didn't know what to make of my dream. On its face, it was odd and disturbing. Ordinarily, Falstaff makes you laugh with him. Gregory's emaciated Falstaff was whistling to keep his courage up. It moved you but didn't make you laugh. My Lord Chief Justice was too ominous. But remember that Queen Elizabeth never asked to see My Lord Chief Justice in another play. The heartening and discouraging were all jumbled together. I didn't try then to sort it all out. It seemed like nothing in comparison with the uncertainties of the Limbo Shift. I just sort of let it all perk in the background.

Finally, I decided I had to talk to Toni. We had something somewhere in between a quarrel and a serious discussion. Like Tall's driving, it veered back and forth all over the road.

Here's a condensed version:

When I got home from work one day, Toni had a soap on the tv and was impatiently going through one of her boxes of pictures cut out of slick magazines. No particular theme. Just a bunch of stuff. It was as if she was looking for inspiration. Or maybe it was just a distraction. She had started trying to break herself of the habit of advising the soap characters how to deal with their lives and maybe this took her mind off the screen.

"I don't want to tell you how to live your life," I stupidly lied. I had Tall's advice in my head; I wanted to plunge in, and this was the first thing it occurred to me to say. "Then don't," she said. I ignored that, determined to make my speech.

"But you just can't go on with the Limbo Shift this way. It's already been a lot of trouble, what with that scene with Small, Adam, and that asshole, and that scene with the biker and Milarepa almost blew up."

"Not really. Bikers aren't that hard to handle."

I still ignored what she said. "It was ok as long as it was just a North Beach thing. But even with you and Badges trying to keep a handle on it, it just keeps drawing more attention."

Toni nodded. "Sort of like it was with Millie at first," she said a little smugly.

"And if it keeps drawing attention, something's going to get out of control. You'll get the Saloon closed."

"You don't know that," she said.

"It's bound to happen somehow, I said."

Toni lost her temper. "Fuck you and your common sense. North Beach isn't common sense. You think I'm like the Good Witch of the South or whatever in the Wizard of Oz? I just click my ruby slippers or something? All of a sudden, I was a Dakini, and I can do things but I don't know exactly what, and I'm just doing my best. You think everything's daylight and common sense, but I do the Limbo Shift at night."

She calmed down a little. "Listen, baby, when I went to see Millie after I died, I didn't know he was going to make me a Dakini. I didn't know what would happen. And then after it happened I still didn't know how to be a Dakini. I thought I was supposed to be a guardian spirit for the people in North Beach somehow, but I didn't have any idea how, so I went off painting in New Mexico. It's a beautiful, weird place in its way, but I didn't know it in my bones the way I do North Beach. Then I saw you in Chicago and came to talk to you. And then I decided I just had to come back to North Beach and see what would happen. And Bill Quack gave me the Limbo Shift. I started doing my dancing and more art. And the art is better because it's coming out of my life and what I'm becoming as a Dakini. I'm still feeling my way. But whatever I'm showing people is something new they haven't seen before. I know you can't be a guardian spirit unless somehow you show people something they haven't seen before."

"It's something they haven't seen before," I said, "but you just don't see all the trouble that will come out of it." As I heard myself saying this, I suddenly thought of how the 60's lunch counter sit-ins had sprung up by surprise and all of a sudden, a movement ignited that had changed my life in ways that were still untwisting. I remembered the chorus of good liberals saying they sympathized with the sit-ins and so forth but deplored the lawlessness and all the trouble it was stirring up. That blind "and so forth" dismissal of what was growing particularly angered me. I now flushed a deep red because I couldn't stand to hear that echo in my words. How could I deny her her struggle?

Toni said. "Look, I really love the way you've been there for me all the time, or almost all the time, even when you were mad at me or it didn't make sense to you. But this stuff is what I am. This is what I know how to do, or, at least, what I'm figuring out to do." And then suddenly, she lost her temper. "So fuck off if you can't take it."

Her Tarot deck was out sitting on a table. I took a deck of regular playing cards out of a drawer, sorted through it to find a joker, showed it to Toni, and put it into her Tarot deck. It was too small, but then so was Toni. "There's always a joker, I guess," I said to her. She made a tight smile at my peace offering.

I leaned forward to kiss her. She hesitated, then kissed me back a little. But noncommittally."

Chapter 14 First Fire: Toni Takes Center Stage

From I don't know when Toni had been a background character for me in the North Beach bars, one of a lot of people with whom I shared a vaguely defined camaraderie. I recall seeing her one time at an outdoor party over in the East Bay, showing off her compact figure in a bikini. I recall talking to her but have no idea any longer what about. It was 1983 when she suddenly took center stage for me.

Indirectly, Candi was the trigger. I had gone with Candi to see the movie, <u>Gandhi</u>. Afterwards we stopped in Vesuvio for a drink. The guy on the stool on the other side of Candi started hitting on her, telling her about how he was a CPA and had just recently opened up his own office around the corner on Pacific Avenue. He complained about the homeless sleeping in the doorway of the office building. "Building security says, 'Talk to the police.' The police say, 'You can file a complaint if you want to, but it won't do any good. Your building security should be able to take care of it.' I go back to building security. They say, 'They're like flies. Roust them, and they just come back.' 'Well, I said, you could hose them down or something. If you did something like that, it might keep them away.' Honestly, these people have no respect for property. They don't care how they can damage my image. Clients don't want to have to walk over homeless people to get to their CPA."

Candi tried to ignore him, but her abstraction just seemed to egg him on. Finally, she tossed down her drink and stormed out of the bar, me following. In the street, she said, "That idiot. What we need is more poor people to keep scum like that out." The two of us went up to her apartment to drink and talk. It wound up a pleasant evening full of back and forth about the movie, the incident at Vesuvio, times past, this and that. At home the next morning, out of nostalgia, I wrote a romantic poem thinking about her and her abstracted dreamy attractiveness:

> As if the wind, for fun, twirled itself around the air
> And there you were, all nerves.
> No wonder no one can ever touch you, love,
> As if you'd, like a bubble, burst.
>
> No, these are pretty figures, love, like yours;
> But what I really think I feel:
> Hunger, eating air, makes a low growling belly.
> The truth is, what's wrong with grass stains.

That day was the annual anniversary party at Specs' bar, where he threw a big feed. I'm always excited about a new piece of verse right after it's written, and I took a few copies to Specs to show off to friends.

Specs was crowded, so after eating, I moved on to the Coffee Gallery. I had a nice buzz on and was playing bridge at the big table in the front window. Back at Specs a friend had shown Toni my poem. Now she came in, rushed up to me, and, waving the copy I'd given away, said, "Wow. I had no idea you had something like that in you." I was surprised and flattered. I pulled her close to me, kissed her, and went on with my game. As I realized later, that had been exactly the right thing to do. Including treating it lightly by going right back to my game. But it led to intense conversations in the bar over the next few days.

Her life was in crisis. Toni showed me a dull-edged cut at the base of her left thumb. "It's from my fingernail cutting into it. I just keep clenching my fist."

Her second marriage, from which she had expected security, had suddenly blown up. Her husband had been a flamboyant man with an expensive home in the East Bay and a big wholesale produce business. Lots of money moving in and out all the time. Then, he was indicted for embezzlement and money laundering. "He'd been tense, but that was the way he was all the time. He was never relaxed. At first, when I met him, I thought he was brilliant and liked his kind of 'Fuck you' attitude to everything. I was in Woey Loy Goey in Chinatown with him one night after the bars closed with some other people. He was buying food for everybody. He started undressing right there at the table, just taking one thing off after another until he was naked. And he just sat there that way, eating his food. There were only a few regulars there, the restaurant people knew him, and he spent a lot of money there, so the waitress and everybody just ignored it. He was brilliant. But he could be a real bastard, too. That's when I got seriously into speed while I was with him. I needed something, and he always had it around. Then everything came down around his head. All of a sudden, he had nothing. He divorced me just before he managed to get away to Mexico. Now I'm back in North Beach with nothing."

The Duke, in the first years I'd known him, when he was out in the bars drunk at night, liked to tear $20 bills into little pieces to show, "Money don't mean nothing to me." He particularly liked to do it when there was a woman close by. I thought it showed more of a kind of love/hate relationship to money, and I thought Toni's ex's showing he could eat naked in the restaurant was more of the same. I told Toni that. It hadn't occurred to her. "I guess maybe so," she said. Then, a moment later, "I wish I'd thought of that before. Maybe it would have made a difference how I looked at him. Doesn't do me any good now, though."

Nostalgic poems about Candi dropped right out of my mind. After one of my intense conversations in the bar with Toni, I wrote the poem below, the first of many I've written of her over the years. The next day, I showed it to her.

Bloodweed

No, not like milkweed, darling,
Bloodweed.
Sweet,
Sweet,
Sweet.

Draw all your complex nature
Through your
Teat,
Teat,
Teat.

But, to break out of this sudden vein, you witch,
With your black, white magic pulsing like Alph, the sacred river,
To the oceans of sleep

I had a dream of you.
I do not know what kind of dream it was.
Deep,
Deep,

Deep.

"It's about you," I told her. "I know," she said. I think this first one stayed her favorite of the things I wrote about her. It was the second time I had done something exactly right. I point these out because it didn't happen so often.

I had a real dream about her. My bridge-playing friend, Larry, also a chess player, had told me one of his dreams once. He saw the ace of spades, the death card, set up on the chess board like a queen, in charge of everything, just like the red queen in <u>Alice Through the Looking Glass</u>. It made me think of how Toni had talked to me about the Tarot deck, and particularly about the Hanged Man in it. "It's the death card, but it's not just negative. It means change." In my dream, I saw Toni smiling at me out of the ace of spades. She was surrounded by flames but not consumed.

She was living then in La Buona Casa, a rooming house above a storefront on Columbus Avenue not far from Washington Square Park. There were some other old-time bar people also there – Caroline, who had loaned Firebird her Medi-Cal card, and Minnie Mack, a sometime restaurant cook or waitress, who had a personality something like a Mack truck. She took a lot of grief over her name.

Toni invited me up to her room. I wondered whether she was inviting me up to "see her etchings," so to speak. It was a small room. We sat together on the bed, which was about the only place where there was any space. The rest was filled with Toni's artwork, some finished, some in progress.

There was a lamp. The bulb went inside a mannequin's empty head. Below the shoulder, the torso had been replaced by a violin.

There was a hawk's wing nailed on the wall. "I saw a jackrabbit kick it off the hawk," she said.

On the wall, there were the India Ink blackbirds I've mentioned and her Madonna.

There were boxes and boxes of magazine pages and other miscellaneous photos and scraps that Toni had stashed for use in collages. There were some collages in progress. "I didn't know you were an artist," I said. "Not enough people do," she said.

Toni stepped into her closet for a moment. I was looking at all her stuff. I looked around as she came back into the room. She had one arm tied off and was sticking a needle into the vein. "I wish I hadn't seen that," I said. "It was time you knew," she said.

She went on to show me photos of Andrew, her young roofer lover. The photos showed him naked, and she was working on a collage using them. She hadn't yet decided how she wanted to put them together or what to put with them. She talked about her fascination with Andrew and his body.

Being all wrapped up in her feelings for Andrew, Toni decided on the spot that I was too old for her, even though five years younger than her, and many, many more than that in sexual experience. Andrew was what was in her mind right now, so she talked to me about it. She hadn't brought me to her room to show me her etchings.

First the kiss in the Coffee Gallery and the intense talks in the days following, then the scene in her room, were like combination punches to me. Someone simultaneously so full of trouble and so full of life and death, both at once, was a shock to me. She was semi-suicidal then and for quite some time after that. If she was down and I tried to comfort her, she would reject it, saying tightly, "I just don't like it here." (Meaning this life.) If I stopped trying to comfort her and went along with her despair, she'd say, "Are you trying to get rid of me?" This was a serious version of the story I heard once about a couple little kids trying to get a parrot perched on a stand to talk. The kids would say phrases to the parrot. The parrot would cock his head and listen but was mute. Finally, the kids gave up and started to walk away. As they turned around, the bird said, "Don't go."

But on the whole, she talked more to me about herself and what was happening to her than I talked about myself. Generally speaking, Toni liked guys strutting themselves to impress her. It was flattering whether she was impressed or not. But right now was a tangled time for her so she had a need to talk – not to get advice but for the resonance talking to somebody gives to you.

I wrote this poem:

Suicide

Your devils hated me because I loved what they despised:
Namely, you.
Therefore, they conspired to take
A world from me
Nothing to them:
Your life.

I quote this mainly for Toni's reaction to it. "I thought they loved me," she said.

She faced her situation not like a heroine on the railroad tracks in a cowboy movie waiting for the hero to come along and untie her, but something like someone in a bad dream hopefully choosing doors one after another in a game show and finding each one leads her back into the same mess.

I recall thinking having Toni penetrate into my life as she had was like stepping on a nail and having it go right through the sole of my shoe and up into my soul. It's not immediately painful. It's a shock. It's unexpected, can't be ignored, is hard to get out, and it immediately changes your life.

CHAPTER 15 THE LIMBO SHIFT COMES TO AN END

Damian was always uneasy with the Limbo Shift. Bill Quack had already been doing it when Nappy had the bar. Damian didn't like the idea from the start, but Bill was so erratic about it, and that made it easier to live with. Bill had never been easy to deal with. Nappy used to keep firing him, then hiring him again after he discovered and rediscovered how the take dropped off when somebody else worked his shifts. Bill told a story about how one time he was working drunk, and Nappy fired him. Bill had all the keys to the place hooked onto his belt. Nappy demanded them. In taking them off his belt, drunk as he was, Bill accidentally spilled them under the duckboards. Nappy, when he grudgingly rehired him a few weeks later, waved a finger in his face and yelled, "But the next time I fire you, goddamnit, don't you never spill them keys."

With Bill a ghost, it made Damian especially uncomfortable. Finally, it was easier just to let Bill keep the Limbo Shift going. Toni made Damian even more uncomfortable. She was not just a ghost but, as he saw it, a sort of dragon as well. Then, despite efforts to keep it quiet, the music always threatened to get publicity outside the neighborhood, jeopardizing his license if it became officially known. But Toni was as careful as she could be about that, and Badges had a cop friend that he pieced off pretty regularly out-of-the-door charges. And there was no getting around it: The Limbo Shift was a money maker. Also, Damian liked the music and had a natural sympathy with musicians.

I've mentioned that Damian had set up a recording studio in the basement where he made CDs of some of the groups that played in the Saloon. They were for sale in the bar. One of the regulars was a semi-pro in making music CDs and videos. One Limbo Shift he made a music video of Jerry C. playing and Toni's color dancing and burned 10 copies in the basement studio. The cover called it "The Graceful Dead – recorded live." It was odd. In the video you could only see a kind of dancing light show. Toni's body was entirely invisible. You could only sort of make out that there was a body there from the way the colors bent around it. The original CDs went to insiders, who were supposed to keep them very quiet. But you know the way the world works. Rumors got around – and different versions kept spreading and changing – and pirate copies started to appear. Damian was at once pissed that the CD had been made and also, at the same time, that he wasn't making any money off all the pirate copies. In the CDs, it wasn't obvious that it had been done at the Saloon, which was a relief to Damian, but he was in no position to sue anybody for the piracy.

Mary Thomas, as I've mentioned, had been a stripper and was proud of the body she'd had in those days and of her dancing. She'd given me photos of herself in the old days, and she truly had had a great curvy body. Now, heading for 60, she still had a nice shape, but not so lithe and moved it a bit heavily. And she had started to grow wrinkles. Especially once she saw the "Graceful Dead" video, she was jealous. "I used to do a routine a lot like that. I made myself a costume with lots of sequins, and the place I danced had one of those disco mirror spheres with flashes of different colored lights reflecting off it. They reflected off me, too. Everybody loved it. Everybody was crazy about me. I got tips like you wouldn't believe."

Toni wasn't too happy with Mary trying to steal her thunder this way. She really wished her body had shown normally in the video, especially her Dakini tail. I tried to calm her by quoting from Andrew Marvell's "Thoughts in a Garden" and its elegant "Annihilating all that's made/To a green thought in a green shade."

"O, yeah?" she said, "What about thoughts in a whorehouse? 'Exhilarating all that's made/To red, red, red, red, red.'"

She decided she wanted to do a collage based on the video. She got the guy who made it to email me a bunch of stills that I could print out from my computer.

It was just about the same time that Toni got her collage idea that Small suffered a terrible blow.

Ever since Texas had left and she had gotten Adam, Adam had given her the faithful, loving companion she needed. Adam went with her everywhere. She couldn't take him into the bars except now and then – depending on who was behind the bar and how busy it was. If Adam couldn't come in, he lay down on the side walk outside until Small came out. One time Adam had been lying down and then casually looked into the Coffee Gallery for Small. He didn't see her. He went up to Green Street and looked in the Columbus Café. No Small. In Gino's. Still no Small. Down Grant to the Saloon. Still no Small. Back to the Coffee Gallery. Still no Small. Adam was starting to freak out. Bill, the Coffee Gallery owner, came out and brought Adam back to his tiny office, opened the door, and showed him Small passed out there. Adam went back outside, lay down, and waited.

One evening, Small was in the Lost and Found with Adam on the sidewalk outside. Small came out to go talk to somebody at the Saloon. This time, Adam didn't notice her leaving. I guess he'd

drowsed off. When Adam woke he looked inside the Lost and
Found but didn't see Small. He circled all through the place a
couple times before he was shooed out. He was standing outside on
the sidewalk, nervous and worried, when he saw Small coming out
of the Saloon. He started to run across the street to Small just when
a BMW was driving by. It hit him hard. He let out a howl and
thumped onto the street. The driver stopped and came out of his
car to check whether it was damaged and cursed at the blood and
fur on his front end. Then he got back in and drove off. Small ran
to Adam and put her arms around his neck. He whimpered and
looked at her pathetically. She called 911. "Adam has been hit by a
car. I think he's maybe dying. You have to send an ambulance
quick." The ambulance arrived. The paramedics, seeing Adam was
a dog, were very nice about it. They donated a stretcher and
carefully lifted Adam onto it. Then, they found the number for the
SPCA vet hospital and called it for Small. Small found a friend
with a pickup truck, and Adam was carefully loaded into the back.
Small rode with him in the back to the vet hospital. But it was all
too late. Adam was 90% gone by the time they got there and was
altogether dead within another half hour.

It's hard to think of anything worse that could have happened
to Small. And the asshole BMW driver inflamed all her
revolutionary ideas, and she ranted constantly about rat pig
capitalists, guns, and revolution. A little later, somebody told
Small they had seen some guy in Vesuvio complaining about how
some stupid dog had run out in front of his new car and put a dent
in it. Telling Small was a stupid, thoughtless thing to do. It only
made her grief and rage worse, and now she was on the lookout in
case the murderer appeared again in North Beach.

I've mentioned that often, the early stages of Toni's work seemed clichéd. Her collage from the video couldn't even really get started. She had cut a piece of cardboard for the backing and kept laying out the video stills – her light show dancing and Jerry C. playing. There had been some other photos of her behind the bar during the Limbo Shift, and in those, her body showed up normally – if you could call her Dakini body normal. She made a bunch of copies of the photos she wanted to use so she would have backups if she damaged one of them in her experiments with them. She tried to use the shots of Jerry C. in combination with the video light show dancing, but it didn't seem to work out. She couldn't find anything that interested her – or me either, though I was wise enough to be noncommittal about what I thought.

At length, she started to break away from that Limbo Shift video stills.

Toni liked to do Tarot layouts, muse over them, and interpret her life through them. For myself, I never had any belief in Tarot fortune telling, but I did believe in Toni's intuitions, which somehow seemed to me to have something to them even when they were wildly unrealistic. I was often tempted to ask her to do a layout for me and interpret it. But I never did. It seemed as if it would have been too disturbing of her image of me to have me wanting into what was a very private ceremony for her. Not to mention what it might end up doing to my image of me.

I had gotten a modernized Tarot deck for her on a vacation in British Columbia. She didn't like it. She preferred the old traditional deck she kept wrapped in a special cloth. She liked particularly to lecture me on the Hanged Man card. "It's not just death," she said, "It's change. It's not just negative. You just don't know exactly what it is. It all depends on what's around it in the layout."

She put the Hanged Man card into her layout, then had me find on the internet an image of Milarepa, all green, in the Lotus position, but leaning forward as if studying something. She positioned him so that he was studying the Hanged Man card.

Jerry C. was a sax player, but she got a picture of an electric guitar such as the one Milarepa had appeared in in the Saloon neon sign. She managed to find a picture of Jerry C. that she could paste the guitar over as if he were playing it. But that still didn't satisfy her. She got a photo of a heart and pasted it over the body of the guitar. Then she got some broken guitar strings from one of the Saloon musicians and pasted one of them over the heart/guitar. She still couldn't find anything that really satisfied her.

Then, one day, she had me find a picture of a volcano crater – just the top with the crater, not the whole mountain --and also an eagle's nest. She put the eagle's nest near the crater, and pasted on it some broken guitar strings as if they were part of the eagle's nest. She put an egg in the nest, cracked open from a hatching. She pasted herself from the light show, dancing stills over the crater. It looked like a strange kind of eruption from the volcano. She put in a fierce looking eagle flying away with a baby gripped in its talons – not piercing the baby but closed all around him. The bar scene had disappeared entirely. Now, there were four things:

- Milarepa studying the Hanged Man;

- Jerry C. and his heart/guitar with the busted string;

- the volcano with its light show/Toni eruption;

• and the eagle's nest with the guitar strings and the eagle flying away with the baby in its talons.

Toni said, "You can't tell whether the eagle is rescuing the baby or if it's just prey for him. To tell that you'd have to see the whole layout. But you can't. This is all you can see."

Small was getting worse, not better after Adam got run over. At times, she blamed herself for leaving Adam by himself outside the Lost and Found. But mostly, she muttered about the rat pig BMW driver. She scarcely left the Crow's Nest, Tall said, and just sat in the window, smoked grass, muttered about the BMW driver, and cried. Tall couldn't stand to be there with her anymore. She'd work her shifts at Vesuvio, hit the other bars, drink until she was ready to pass out, then go home oblivious to everything. "I don't know how long I'll be able to take this. I don't know what to do. I mean, I'm sorry for Small. But I just can't keep on taking this."

Toni was excited about completing her collage and was going to show it off on the Limbo Shift as she'd done with her Opportunity Mask. She could hardly wait. She went in early, just around the last call, and started to set up. The new collage – she didn't have a title yet – was propped up on a chair in the back and roped off.

Small had come out of the Crow's Nest for some groceries from the little Korean store on Grant and Green, the only one still open at that hour. Coming back by the Lost and Found, she looked in the window and thought she saw the BMW driver. She dropped her groceries and headed immediately for Red's room at the Tower Hotel. He wasn't there, but she still had his keys and got his revolver. She hurried back to the Lost and Found and went in, but once she got a close look at the guy there, she realized it wasn't the

BMW driver. "You're the wrong one," she said. Then, a couple seconds later, "Lucky for you."

She left and, almost automatically, out of habit, headed for the Saloon. There were only a handful of people there. Toni was finishing setting up her collage. Badges was helping her and Jerry C., a couple other musicians, and a Limbo Shift irregular were watching. Toni had started explaining her collage. Small came in the door, unconscious that she had the revolver in her hand. Badges came toward her. "Alice, you can't come in here like that. Let me take you back to the Crow's Nest." He started to put his hand on her shoulder. It never entered his mind that he could be in any danger from Small.

"You can't tell me what to do," she screamed. "This is my place. This is my home." And she emptied the revolver into him. Badges grunted and fell to the floor, bleeding all over. Small, in a daze, seeing what she'd done, dropped the revolver and ran out the door.

Toni turned an ugly, bloated crimson all over to see Badges murdered again, this time, if not exactly by an old friend, at least by someone he, she, and all of us had known in all her comings and goings for years and years. Toni then went black, then mottled black and purple. She came from behand the bar and stood near the door where Badges was bleeding just inside. She started getting ugly yellow patches, also. She was like a full-body bruise. Then, gradually, all those ugly spots and patches started turning a deep indigo as if ink were gradually seeping into them. She herself became less defined, as if the ink were seeping all through her and out of her. There was nothing for anybody to do, say, think, or feel. In shock, everybody just stood there. Then Milarepa appeared in the Budweiser sign for a second only before the whole sign shattered onto the floor with a loud electric screech and pop. Gradually, standing in the dark open doorway, Toni melted away, Toni the Dakini, Toni the artist, Toni the woman, Toni the do/don't girl, stirring things up, solving nothing, erratic as Milarepa's buzzing and popping neon sign had been-- if you knew her, you really loved her… disappearing up into the starry sky, that great celestial river at once infinitely near and far, touching each inside and out. Did Toni save the people of North Beach? Well, no, but Toni the Dakini showed everybody who saw her something they'd never seen before, something for them to work with. Toni had a vision. That, to me, is suchness.

And this book, such as it is, is my gift to you.

APPENDIX: THE BARS AND PEOPLE OF NORTH BEACH

Map of North Beach Where All This Stuff Took Place

Not everything on this map was there at the same time. This is sort of a map of my memory of North Beach.

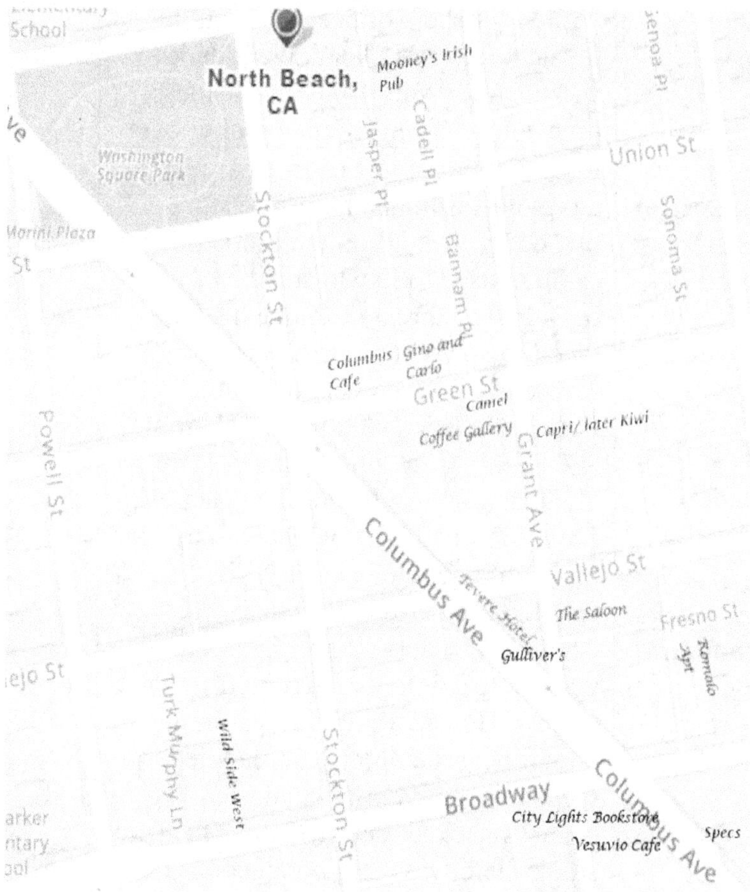

Bars: These Were Our Living Rooms	
The Saloon	Full name: 1232 Fresno Hotel Saloon. Perhaps the oldest bar in San Francisco. Water permit going back to 1860's. When I first came to North Beach in 1970, there were old easy chairs in the back and old Italians on the bar stools. Then Nappy took it over, and it became a North Beach Bohemian bar. Happy hour 8-9 pm with $1 pitchers of beer. Brought in music a few years later. Went dark for a while after Nappy put his business up his nose. Then Damian took it over.
Coffee Gallery/Lost and Found	Right next door to Figoni's hardware, a big old-fashioned hardware store owned by two old Italian brothers. One of them used to like to stand just outside the store and smoke his pipe. One time a young tourist was staring reverently into the window of the Coffee Gallery. She turned to Figoni and said, "Wow. I understand Allen Ginsburg and, Bob Kaufman, and even Janis Joplin all here. Right?" Figoni took a moment to answer, "Uh… … … This is a hardware store."
Gino and Carlo	Charles McCabe, a San Francisco <u>Chronicle</u> columnist, used to drink at Gino's. He had a favorite seat in the corner near the door. After he died, there was a memorial at Gino's. The bar was packed. On McCabe's favorite stool, there was a big bouquet of flowers. One of the Italian regulars

	came in, looked around, and saw every other stool was taken. He unceremoniously lifted the bouquet off the stool, set it on the floor right beside him, sat down, and ordered his drink
Columbus	I used to pass the Columbus Café regularly on my way to work. There was an old guy I'd regularly see sitting on a stool near the window, slumped over his drink. One time, they had to call an ambulance for a customer who'd fainted in the back of the bar. The paramedics, when they arrived, headed straight for the guy in the window to put him on their stretcher.
Specs	Directly across Columbus from Vesuvio and City Lights bookstore. The bartender had cards available to advise customers on courtesy. The one given to women said, "The gentleman would prefer to sulk in silence." Don't recall what the one given to men said.
Vesuvio	My spot for morning coffee for many years. They regularly had art displays along the wall. One time, there was an empty slot in a display where a painting had been sold. I got them to put Toni's <u>Madonna</u> there for the rest of that show.
Gullivers	My spot for weekend mornings. Dolly made eggs/omelets out of an electric frying pan, then.
Mooney's Irish pub	On upper Grant north of Union. Bill from the Coffee Gallery had it for a time after he sold the Coffee Gallery.

Capri/Kiwi	The Capri was a gay bar. The new owner, a short-tempered ex-merchant seaman, renamed it the Kiwi. The new owner was the only bar owner I've come across whose own bartenders refused to serve him. Too much of a troublemaker.
Wumper's	Succeeded another bar whose name I can't remember. Had some good music, but didn't last that long. I went to its opening party.
Blanco's	On Kearny just around the corner from Columbus. Owner and bartender a Chinese former merchant seaman. A bit deaf from holding a firecracker too close to his face to see why it hadn't exploded. It exploded.

People: My North Beach Extended Family	
Crystal Ball	Young topless dancer with a gorgeous figure. Toni and I put her up briefly in the Romolo apartment while she was quarreling with her old man at the time. Later, she got Toni a place to stay for a little while, right after Toni's mastectomy.
Dolly	One of my very good friends in North Beach. A bartender and jack of all trades.
Bill Quack	Free-wheeling North Beach bartender who loved to stir things up. Got his nickname because he liked to do Donald Duck-type excited quacks. During his life founded the Limbo Shift, a totally unauthorized after-closing time shift at the Saloon. Continued it after his death until turning it over to Toni.

The Allice – Alice Tall	The senior half of the Alice. Experienced, big heart, worked an early morning shift at Vesuvio's. Shared the Crow's Nest, a small hotel room at the Tevere Hotel with a big bay window looking out over the Columbus/Broadway intersection on one side and upper Grant Avenue and the Saloon on the other.
The Alice – Alice Small	Small and slender. I think Filipino and Native American blood. Cleaned rooms, swamped bars, genius dumpster diver. Easily impressed by self-important men.
Firebird	Morning bartender at the Vesuvio and later at Gullivers. A big, swaggering redhead from Phoenix. But don't call her "Phoenix," it's "Firebird."
Badges	Doorman at the Coffee Gallery on music nights. Later, doorman on Toni's Limbo Shift.
Damian	Owner of the Saloon after Nappy. Musician and son in the Chinese family that owned the building where the Saloon stood.
Nappy	Owner of the Saloon. Changed it from a place where old Italians hung out to a busy hang-out for a Bohemian crowd. Later, part owner of the Coffee Gallery. Introduced music at the Saloon. Very short and aggressive temperament.
Mel	Became a good friend from sitting on the next bar stool when having my early morning coffee. Merchant seaman and wide reader.
Wes	Drunk and dirty old man par excellence. Loved to stir up an argument but more for the fun and the challenge of the duel than from ill nature.

Candi	A fairly brief romance until she got a Post Office job and settled her life a bit. But a good friend romance or not.
The Duke	"King of the Road" is running a parking lot on Broadway. Not much space, so he had to shuffle the cars in and out of spaces on the street. Loved spending in the bars and going to the crap house.
Billboard Fred	Nickname from his job putting up billboard ads. But also made some money from his paintings. Quiet but could put in a needle. Once saw him listening to an attractive but hard-looking blonde who was declaiming to him, "I just got out of Rikers Island. I am a poet. My book is called <u>Eat Your Babies While Their Bones Are Soft</u>." Fred just quietly asked her, "And what are you going to call your next book."
Captain Marvelous	Always saying "Marvelous" Affected manner. To my surprise, I discovered he had put together a really good art collection from various North Beach artists. The collection I saw, he told me, was a replacement for what had been burned in a fire some years ago.
Old Larry	Chess player, bridge player, and drunk. Once held responsible computer job but long before I knew him. Good friend.
Big Dan	Another guy who had once had a responsible computer job but gave up the working world for Bohemia. Just slightly older than me I think. Didn't drink much. Played excellent chess and learned to play excellent bridge. Good friend.
Big Will	About 6'6", a former longshoreman whose regular working life had been ended by an injury long before I knew him. Lived at

	Project Artaud, an artist's colony in an old warehouse. Painted big abstract acrylics in which he often dripped on the paint, then turned the canvas to redirect the dripping. Also made buttons from different colored clays that he molded together with his hands, then fired, then tumbled for a day or so to make them smooth. They looked sort of like river pebbles. Gave lots of strength to his great big hands.
Ed and Jennie	Ed I knew from the bridge table. Quiet and capable. Hooked up with Jennie, a cocktail waitress with a couple kids. Together they put together a business hauling junk, then selling what was salvageable in a small thrift store out in the Mission.
Lena	A blues singer who could really belt it out. And sometime early morning bartender at the Saloon. Good friend.
Leon	Used to declaim his poetry at Coffee Gallery poetry readings. Quite short and quite loud. Leon, not the name his mother gave him. From Leon Trotsky – "I am the revolution."
Red	Intelligent but doctrinaire with a love of gun rights
Mary Thomas	Long ago, a stripper, now hopelessly hopeful about attracting a good stud. Near sighted but practiced in building doll house models and sewing. Made my Superman-style Rainier Ale cape for me to wear on Halloween.
Gil	Even-tempered bartender at the Coffee Gallery. About 6'5", so he rarely got opposition when he asked somebody to leave. Told me about a tourist who hadn't tipped at all asked when ordering his fifth beer, "Doesn't this bar ever buy a drink?" Gil

	answered, "I really don't know, sir. I've only worked here two years."
Karl	Owner of the Coffee Gallery when I started drinking there. Loved to play liar's dice. Story has it that he won the Coffee Gallery from Annie Watson playing dice.
Annie Watson	Tough old bull dyke but a good sort. I used to amuse/annoy her by calling her Sweet Talking Annie.
Crazy Old Pete	He and his dog lived in the same hotel as old Larry for a time. Later, out in the street. Used to spare change people on the corner of Broadway and Columbus and sleep in Adler Alley beside City Lights bookstore. One time, he asked me for spare change. "Sorry, Pete, I can't do it today," I said. "You need some?" he asked. Someone told me they had seen him one night get out of a cab outside City Lights bookstore, pay the cabbie, then lie down in the alley to go to sleep.

ABOUT THE AUTHOR

It is an ancient Mariner,
And he stoppeth one of three.
'By thy long grey beard and glittering eye,
Now wherefore stopp'st thou me?

…

He holds him with his skinny hand,
'There was a ship,' quoth he.
'Hold off! Unhand me, grey-beard loon!'
Eftsoons his hand dropt he.

He holds him with his glittering eye—

> *Rime of the Ancient Mariner, Samuel Taylor Coleridge*

> *The author has put all he has learned on the seas of life into this tale.*

The author, a Common Bohemian Greybeard Loon, in his native habitat.

www.ingramcontent.com/pod-product-compliance
Lightning Source LLC
Chambersburg PA
CBHW060448310726
48977CB00001B/366